# Two Strangers by Margaret Oliphant

Margaret Oliphant Wilson was born on April 4th, 1828 to Francis W. Wilson, a clerk, and Margaret Oliphant, at Wallyford, near Musselburgh, East Lothian.

Her youth was spent in establishing a writing style and by 1849 she had her first novel published: Passages in the Life of Mrs. Margaret Maitland.

Two years later, in 1851 Caleb Field was published and also an invitation gained to contribute to Blackwood's Magazine; the beginning of a lifelong business relationship.

In May 1852, Margaret married her cousin, Frank Wilson Oliphant. Their marriage produced six children but, tragically, three died in infancy. When her husband developed signs of the dreaded consumption (tuberculosis) they moved to Florence, and then to Rome where, sadly, he died.

Margaret was naturally devastated but was also now left without support and only her income from writing to support the family. She returned to England and took up the burden of supporting her three remaining children by her literary activity.

Her incredible and prolific work rate increased both her commercial reputation and the size of her reading audience. Tragedy struck again in January 1864 when her only remaining daughter, Maggie, died.

In 1866 she settled at Windsor to be closer to her sons, who were being educated at near-by Eton School.

For more than thirty years she pursued a varied literary career but family life continued to bring problems. Cyril Francis, her eldest son, died in 1890. The younger son, Francis, who she nicknamed 'Cecco', died in 1894.

With the last of her children now lost to her, she had little further interest in life. Her health steadily and inexorably declined.

Margaret Oliphant Wilson Oliphant died at the age of 69 in Wimbledon on 20th June 1897. She is buried in Eton beside her sons.

## Index of Contents

CHAPTER IX
MARGARET OLIPHANT - A SHORT BIOGRAPHY
MARGARET OLIPHANT - A CONCISE BIBLIOGRAPHY


CHAPTER I

"And who is this young widow of yours whom I hear so much about? I understand Lucy's rapture over any stranger; but you, too, mother—"

"I too—well, there is no particular witchcraft about it; a nice young woman has as much chance with me as with any one, Ralph—"

"Oh, if it's only a nice young woman"—

"It's a great deal more," said Lucy. "Why, Miss Jones at the school is a nice young woman—don't you be taken in by mother's old-fashioned stilts. She is a darling—she is as nice as nice can be. She's pretty, and she's good, and she's clever. She has read a lot, and seen a lot, and been everywhere, and knows heaps and heaps of people, and yet just as simple and as nice as if she had never been married, never had a baby, and was just a girl like the rest of us—Mother! there is nothing wrong in what I said?" Lucy suddenly cried, stopping short and blushing all over with the innocent alarm of a youthfulness which had not been trained to modern modes of speech.

"Nothing wrong, certainly," said the mother, with a half smile; "but—there is no need for entering into all these details."

"They would have found out immediately, though," said Lucy, with a lowered voice, "that there was—Tiny, you know."

The scene was a drawing-room in a country house looking out upon what was at this time of year the rather damp and depressing prospect of a park, with some fine trees and a great breadth of very green, very mossy, very wet grass. It was only October, though the end of the month; and in the middle of the day, in the sunshine, the trees, in all their varied colors, were a fine sight, cheerful and almost exhilarating, beguiling the eye; but now the sun was gone, the leaves were falling in little showers whenever the faintest breath of air arose, and where the green turf was not veiled by their many colored remnants, it was green with that emerald hue which means only wet; one knew as one gazed across it that one's foot would sink in the spongy surface, and wet, wet would be the boot, the skirt which touched it; the men in their knickerbockers, or those carefully turned up trousers—which we hear are the fashion in the dryest streets of Paris and New York—suffered comparatively little. The brushwood was all wet, with blobs of moisture on the long brambles and drooping leaves. The park was considered a beautiful park, though not a very large one, but it was melancholy itself to look out for hours together upon that green expanse in such an evening. It was not a bad evening either. There was no rain; the clouds hung low, but as yet had given forth no shower. The air was damp but yet brisk. There was a faint yellow glimmer of what might have been sunset in the sky.

The windows in the Wradisley drawing-rooms were large; one of them, a vast, shallow bow, which seemed to admit the outside into the interior, rather than to enlighten the interior with the view of what was outside. Mrs. Wradisley sat within reach of, but not too near, a large, very red fire—a fire which was like the turf outside, the growth of generations, or at least had not at all the air of having been lighted to-day or any recent day. It did not flame, but glowed steadily, adding something to the color of the room, but not much to the light. Later in the season, when larger parties assembled, there was tea in the hall for the sportsmen and the ladies who waited for them; but Mrs. Wradisley thought the hall draughty, and much preferred the drawing-room, which was over-furnished after the present mode of drawing-rooms, but at least warm, and free from draughts. She was working—knitting with white pins, or else making mysterious chains and bridges in white wool with a crochet-hook, her eyes being supposed to be not very strong, and this kind of industry the best adapted for them. As to what Lucy was doing, that defies description. She was doing everything and nothing. She had something of a modern young lady's contempt for every kind of needlework, and, then, along with that, a great admiration for it as something still more superior than the superiority of idleness. A needle is one of the things that has this double effect. It is the scorn of a great number of highly advanced, very cultured and superior feminine people; but yet here and there will arise one, still more advanced and cultured, who loves the old-fashioned weapon, and speaks of it as a sacred implement of life. Lucy followed first one opinion and then another. She had half a dozen pieces of work about, begun under the influence of one class of her friends, abandoned under that of another. She had a little studio, too, where she painted and carved, and executed various of the humbler decorative arts, which, perhaps, to tell the truth, she enjoyed more than art proper; but these details of the young lady's life may be left to show themselves where there is no need of such vanities. Lucy was, at all events, whatever her other qualities might be, a most enthusiastic friend.

"Well, I suppose we shall see her, and find out, as Lucy says, for ourselves—not that it is of much importance," the brother said, who had begun this conversation.

"Oh! but it is of a great deal of importance," cried Lucy. "Mrs. Nugent is my chief friend. She is mother's prime favorite. She is the nicest person in the neighborhood. She is here constantly, or I am there. If you mean not to like her, you might as well, without making any fuss about it, go away."

"Lucy!" cried Mrs. Wradisley, moved to indignation, and dropping all the white fabric of wool on her knees, "your brother—and just come home after all these years!"

"What nonsense! Of course I don't mean that in the least," Lucy cried. "Ralph knows—of course, I would rather have him than—all the friends in the world."

There was a faltering note, however, in this profession. Why should she like Ralph better than all the friends in the world? He was her brother, that was true; but he knew very little of Lucy, and Lucy knew next to nothing of him; he had been gone since she was almost a child—he came back now with a big beard and a loud voice and a step which rang through the house. It was evident he thought her, if not a child, yet the most unimportant feminine person who did not count; and why should she prefer him to her own nice friends, who were soft of voice and soft of step, and made much of her, and thought as she did? It is acknowledged universally that in certain circumstances, when the man is her lover, a girl prefers that man to all the rest of the creation; but why, when it is only your brother Raaf, and it may really be said that you don't know him—why should you prefer him to your own beloved friends? Lucy did not ask herself this question—she said what she knew it was the right thing to say, though with a faltering in her voice. And Ralph, who fortunately did not care in the least, took no notice of what Lucy said. He liked the little girl, his little sister, well enough; but it did not upset the equilibrium of the world in the very least whether she preferred him or not—if he had thought on the subject he would probably have said, "More shame to her, the little insensible thing!" but he did not take the trouble to give it a passing thought.

"I've got to show Bertram the neighborhood," he said; "let him see we're not all muffs or clowns in the country. He has a kind of notion that is about what the English aborigines are—and I daresay it's true, more or less."

"Oh, Raaf!" cried Lucy, raising her little smooth head.

"Well, it's natural enough. One doesn't meet the cream of the cream in foreign parts; unless you're nothing but a sportsman, or a great swell doing it as the right thing, the most of the fellows you meet out there are loafers or blackguards, more or less."

"It is a pity to form an estimate from blackguards," said Mrs. Wradisley, with a smile; "but that, I suppose, I may take as an exaggeration too. We don't see much of that kind here. Mr. Bertram is much mistaken if he thinks—"

"Oh, don't be too hasty, mother," said Ralph. "We know the breed; our respectable family has paid toll to the devil like other folks since it began life, which is rather a long time ago. After a few hundred years you get rather proud of your black sheep. I'm something of the kind myself," he added, in his big voice.

Mrs. Wradisley once more let the knitting drop in her lap. "You do yourself very poor justice, Raaf—no justice at all, in fact. You are not spotless, perhaps, but I hope that black—"

"Whitey-brown," said her son. "I don't care for the distinction; but one white flower is perhaps enough in a family that never went in for exaggerated virtue—eh? Ah, yes—I know."

These somewhat incoherent syllables attended the visible direction of Mrs. Wradisley's eyes toward the door, with the faintest lifting of her eyelids. The door had opened and some one had come in. And yet it is quite inadequate to express the entrance of the master of the house by such an expression. His foot made very little sound, but this was from some quality of delicacy and refinement in his tread, not from any want of dignity or even impressiveness in the man. He was dressed just like the other men so far as appeared—in a grey morning suit, about which there was nothing remarkable. Indeed, it would have been against the perfection of the man had there been anything remarkable in his dress—but it was a faultless costume, whereas theirs were but common coats and waistcoats from the tailor's, lined and creased by wear and with marks in them of personal habit, such, for instance, as that minute burnt spot on Raaf's coat-pocket, which subtly announced, though it was a mere speck, the thrusting in of a pipe not entirely extinguished, to that receptacle. Mr. Wradisley, I need not say, did not smoke; he did not do anything to disturb the perfect outline of an accomplished gentleman, refined and fastidious, which was his natural aspect. To smell of tobacco, or indeed of anything, would have put all the fine machinery of his nature out of gear. He hated emotion as he hated—what shall I say?—musk or any such villainous smell; he was always point devise, body and soul. It is scarcely necessary to say that he was Mr. Wradisley and the head of the house. He had indeed a Christian name, by which he was called by his mother, brother, and sister, but not conceivably by any one else. Mr. Wradisley was as if you had said Lord, when used to him—nay, it was a little more, for lord is tant soit peu vulgar and common as a symbol of rank employed by many other people, whereas Mr., when thus elevated, is unique; the commonest of addresses, when thus sublimated and etherealized, is always the grandest of all. He was followed into the room by a very different person, a person of whom the Wradisley household did not quite know what to make—a friend of Ralph's who had come home with him from the deserts and forests whence that big sportsman and virtuous prodigal had come. This stranger's name was Bertram. He had not the air of the wilds about him as Ralph Wradisley had. He was said to be a bigger sportsman even than Ralph, and a more prodigious traveler; but this was only Ralph's report, who was always favorable to his friends; and Mr. Bertram looked more like a man about town than an African traveler, except that he was burnt very brown by exposure, which made his complexion, once fair, produce a sort of false effect in contrast with his light hair, which the sun had rather diminished than increased in color. Almost any man would have looked noisy and rough who had the disadvantage to come into a room after Mr. Wradisley; but Bertram bore the comparison better than most. Ralph Wradisley had something of the aspect of a gamekeeper beside both of them, though I think the honest fellow would have been the first to whom a child or injured person would have turned. The ladies made involuntary mental comments upon them as the three stood together.

"Oh, if Raaf were only a little less rough!" his mother breathed in her heart. Lucy, I think, was most critical of Bertram, finding in him, on the whole, something which neither of her brothers possessed, though he must have been forty at the very least, and therefore capable of exciting but little interest in a girl's heart.

"I have been showing your friend my treasures," said Mr. Wradisley, with a slight turn of his head toward his brother, "and I am delighted to find we have a great many tastes in common. There is a charm in sympathy, especially when it is so rare, on these subjects."

"You could not expect Raaf to know about your casts and things, Reginald," said Mrs. Wradisley, precipitately. "He has been living among such very different scenes."

"Raaf!" said Mr. Wradisley, slightly elevating his eyebrows. "My dear mother, could you imagine I was referring in any way to Raaf?"

"Never mind, Reg, I don't take it amiss," said the big sportsman, with a laugh out of his beard.

There was, however, a faint color on his browned cheeks. It is well that a woman's perceptions should be quick, no doubt, but if Mrs. Wradisley had not been jealous for her younger son this very small household jar need not have occurred. Mr. Wradisley put it right with his natural blandness.

"We all have our pet subjects," he said; "you too, mother, as much as the worst of us. Is the time of tea over, or may I have some?"

"Mr. Wradisley's casts are magnificent," cried the stranger. "I should have known nothing about them but for a wild year or two I spent in Greece and the islands. A traveler gets a sniff of everything. Don't you recollect, Wradisley, the Arabs and their images at—"

The name was not to be spelt by mere British faculties, and I refrain.

"Funny lot of notions," said Raaf, "I remember; pretty little thing or two, however, I should like to have brought for Lucy—just the things a girl would like—but Bertram there snapped them all up before I had a chance—confounded knowing fellow, always got before me. You come down on him, Lucy; it's his fault if I have so few pretty things for you."

"I am very well contented, Raaf," said Lucy, prettily. As a matter of fact the curiosities Ralph had brought home had been chiefly hideous ivory carvings of truly African type, which Lucy, shuddering, had put away in a drawer, thanking him effusively, but with averted eyes.

"There were two or three very pretty little Tanagra figurine among the notions," said Bertram. "I am sorry Miss Wradisley had not her share of them—they're buried in my collections in some warehouse or other, and probably will never see the light."

"Ah, Tanagra!" said Mr. Wradisley, with a momentary gleam of interest. He laid his hand not unkindly on his little sister's shoulder, as she handed him, exactly as he liked it, his cup of tea. "It is the less matter, for Lucy would not have appreciated them," he said.

"When," said Mrs. Wradisley, with a little gasp, "do you expect your friends, Reginald? October is getting on, and the ladies that belong to them will lie heavy on our hands if we have bad weather."

"Oh, the guns," said Mr. Wradisley. "Don't call them my friends, mother—friends of the house, friends of the covers, if you like. Not so great a nuisance as usual this year, since Raaf is here, but no intimates of mine."

"We needn't stand upon words, Reginald. They are coming, anyhow, and I never remember dates."

"Useless to attempt it. You should make a memorandum of everything, which is much more sure. I can tell you at once."

He took a note-book from his pocket, unerringly, without the usual scuffle to discover in which pocket it was, and, drawing a chair near his mother, began to read out the names of the guests. Then there ensued a little discussion as to where they were to be placed; to Mrs. Wradisley proposing the yellow room for one couple who had already, in Mr. Wradisley's mind, been settled in the green. It was not a very great difference, but the master of the house had his way. A similar little argument, growing fainter and fainter on the mother's side, was carried on over the other names. In every case Mr. Wradisley had his way.

"I am going to run down to the park gates—that is, to the village,—I mean I am going to see Mrs. Nugent," said Lucy, "while mother and Reginald settle all these people. Raaf, will you come?"

"And I, too?" said Bertram, with a pleasant smile. He had a pleasant smile, and he was such a gentleman, neither rough like Raaf, nor over-dainty like Reginald. Lucy was very well content he should come too.


CHAPTER II

It was a lingering and pleasant walk with many little pauses in it and much conversation. Lucy was herself the cause of some of them, for it was quite necessary that here and there Mr. Bertram should be made to stop, turn round, and look at the view. I will not pretend that those views were any very great things. Bertram, who had seen all the most famous scenes of earth, was not much impressed by that point so dear to the souls of the Wradisbury people, where the church tower came in, or that other where the glimmer of the pond under the trees, reflecting all their red and gold, moved the natives to enthusiasm. It was a pretty, soft, kindly English landscape, like a good and gentle life, very reposeful and pleasant to see, but not dramatic or exciting. It was Ralph, though he was to the manner born, who was, or pretended to be, the most impatient of these tame but agreeable vistas. "It don't say much, your landscape, Lucy," he said. "Bertram's seen everything there is to see. A stagnant pool and a church tower are not so grand to him as to—" Probably he intended to say us, with a little, after all, of the native's proud depreciation of a scene which, though homely, appeals to himself so much; but he stopped, and wound up with "a little ignoramus like you."

"I am not so fastidious, I suppose. I think it's delightful," said Bertram. "After all the dissipations of fine scenery, there's nothing like a home landscape. I've seen the day when we would have given all we possessed for a glimmer of a church tower, or, still better, a bit of water. In the desert only to think of that would be a good thing."

"Oh, in the desert," said Ralph, with a sort of indulgent acknowledgment that in some points home did commend itself to the most impartial mind. But he too stopped and called upon his friend to observe where the copse spread dark into the sunset sky—the best covert within twenty miles—about which also Bertram was very civil, and received the information with great interest. "Plenty of wild duck round the corner of that hill in the marshy part," said Ralph. "By Jove! we should have a heavy bag when we have it all to ourselves."

"Capital ground, and great luck to be the first," said Mr. Bertram. He was certainly a nice man. He seemed to like to linger, to talk of the sunset, to enjoy himself in the fresh but slightly chill air of the October evening. Lucy's observation of him was minute. A little wonder whether he might be the man—not necessarily her man, but the ideal man—blew like a quiet little breeze through her youthful spirit. It was a breeze which, like the actual breeze of the evening, carried dead leaves with it, the rags of past reputation and visions, for already Lucy had asked herself this question in respect to one or two other men who had not turned out exactly as at first they seemed. To be sure, this one was old—probably forty or so—and therefore was both better and worse than her previous studies; for at such an age he must of course have learnt everything that experience could teach, and on the other hand did not matter much, having attained to antiquity. Still, it certainly gave a greater interest to the walk that he was here.

"After all," said Ralph, "you gave us no light, Lucy, as to who this widow was."

"You speak as if she were like old Widow Thrapton in the village," cried Lucy. "A widow!—she says it's a term of reproach, as if a woman had tormented her husband to death."

"But she is a widow, for you said so—and who is she?" said the persistent Ralph.

"He is like the little boy in 'Helen's Babies,'" said Lucy, turning to her other companion. "He always wants to see the wheels go round, whatever one may say."

"I feel an interest in this mysterious widow, too," said Bertram, with a laugh.

It was all from civility to keep Ralph in countenance, she felt sure.

"Who is she?" said that obstinate person.

"I can tell you what she is," cried Lucy, with indignant warmth. "She must be older than I am, I suppose, for there's Tiny, but she doesn't look it. She has the most lovely complexion, and eyes like stars, and brown hair—none of your golden stuff, which always looks artificial now. Hers might be almost golden if she liked, but she is not one to show off. And she is the nicest neighbor that ever was—comes up to the house just when one is dull and wants stirring up, or sends a note or a book, or to ask for something. She likes to do all sorts of things for you, and she's so generous and nice and natural that she likes you to do things for her, which is so much, much more uncommon! She says, thank heaven, she is not unselfish; and, though it sounds strange," said Lucy, with vehemence, "I know exactly what she means."

"Not unselfish?" said Ralph. "By George! that's a new quality. I thought it was always the right thing to say of a woman that she was unselfish; but all that doesn't throw any light upon the lady. Isn't she somebody's sister or cousin or aunt? Had she a father, had she a mother?—that sort of thing, you know. A woman doesn't come and settle herself in a neighborhood without some credentials—nor a man either, so far as I know."

"I don't know what you mean by credentials. She was not introduced to us by any stupid people, if that is what you mean. We just found her out for ourselves."

Ralph gave a little whistle at this, which made Lucy very angry. "When you go out to Africa or—anywhere," she cried, "do you take credentials? And who is to know whether you are what you call yourself? I suppose you say you're a Wradisley of Wradisbury. Much the black kings must know about a little place in Hants!"

"The black kings don't stand on that sort of thing," said Ralph, "but the mother does, or so I supposed."

"I ought to take the unknown lady's part," said Mr. Bertram. "You've all been very kind to me, and I'm not a Bertram of—anywhere in particular. I have not got a pedigree in my pocket. Perhaps I might have some difficulty in making out my family tree."

"Oh, Mr. Bertram!" cried Lucy, in deprecation, as if that were an impossible thing.

"I might always call myself of the Ellangowan family, to be sure," he said, with a laugh.

Now Lucy did not at all know what he meant by the Ellangowan family. She was not so deeply learned in her Scott as I hope every other girl who reads this page is, and she was not very quick, and perhaps would not have caught the meaning if she had been ever so familiar with "Guy Mannering." She thought Ellangowan a very pretty name, and laid it up in her memory, and was pleased to think that Mr. Bertram had thus, as it were, produced his credentials and named his race. I don't know whether Ralph also was of the same opinion. At all events they went on without further remark on this subject. The village lay just outside the park gates on the right side of a pretty, triangular bit of common, which was almost like a bit of the park, with little hollows in it filled with a wild growth of furze and hawthorn and blackberry, the long brambles arching over and touching the level grass. There was a pretty bit of greensward good for cricket and football, and of much consequence in the village history. The stars had come out in the sky, though it was still twilight when they emerged from the shadow of the trees to this more open spot; and there were lights in the cottage windows and in the larger shadow of the rectory, which showed behind the tall, slim spire of the church. It was a cheerful little knot of human life and interest under the trees, Nature, kindly but damp, mantling everything with greenness up to the very steps of the cottage doors, some of which were on the road itself without any interval of garden; and little irregular gleams of light indicating the scarcely visible houses. Lucy, however, did not lead the way toward the village. She went along the other side of the common toward a house more important than the cottages, which stood upon a little elevation, with a grassy bank and a few moderate-sized trees.

"Oh, she's in Greenbank, this lady," said Ralph. "I thought the old doctor was still there."

"He died last year, after Charlie died at sea—didn't you know? He never held up his head, Raaf, after Charlie died."

"The more fool he; Charlie drained him of every penny, and was no credit to him in any way. He should have been sent about his business years ago. So far as concerned him, I always thought the doctor very weak."

"Oh, Raaf, he was his only son!"

"What then? You think it's only that sort of relationship that counts. The doctor knew as well as any one what a worthless fellow he was."

"But he never held up his head again," said Lucy, "after Charlie died."

"That's how nature confutes all your philosophy, Wradisley," said the other man. "That is the true tragedy of it. Worthy or unworthy, what does it matter? Affection holds its own."

"Oh, I've no philosophy," said Ralph, "only common sense. So they sold the house! and I suppose the poor old doctor's library and his curiosities, and everything he cared for? I never liked Carry. She would have no feeling for what he liked, poor old fellow. Not worth much, that museum of his—good things and bad things, all pell-mell. Of course she sold them all?"

"The most of them," Lucy confessed. "What could she do otherwise, Raaf? They were of no use to her. She could not keep up the house, and she had no room for them in her own. Poor Carry, he left her very little; and her husband has a great struggle, and what could she do?"

"I don't suppose she wanted to do anything else," said Ralph, in a surly tone. "Look here, I sha'n't go in with you since it's the doctor's house. I had a liking for the old fellow—and Bertram and I are both smoking. We'll easy on a bit till the end of the common, and wait for you coming back."

"If you prefer it, Raaf," Lucy said, with a small tone of resignation. She stood for a moment in the faint twilight and starlight, holding her head a little on one side with a wistful, coaxing look. "I did wish you to see her," she said.

"Oh, I'll see her some time, I suppose. Come, Bertram; see you're ready, Lucy, by the time we get back."

Lucy still paused a moment as they swung on with the scent of their cigars sending a little warmth into the damp air. She thought Mr. Bertram swayed a little before he joined the other, as if he would have liked to stay. Undeniably he was more genial than Raaf, more ready to yield to what she wanted. And usually she was alone in her walks, just a small woman about the road by herself, so that the feeling of leading two men about with her was pleasant. She regretted they did not come in to show Mrs. Nugent how she had been accompanied. She went slowly up the grassy bank alone, thinking of this. She had wanted so much to show Raaf to Mrs. Nugent, not, she fancied, that it was at all likely they would take to each other. Nelly Nugent was so quick, she would see through him in a moment. She would perceive that there was not, perhaps, a great deal in him. He was not a reader, nor an artist, nor any of the things Nelly cared for—only a rough fellow, a sportsman, and rather commonplace in his mind. He was only Raaf, say what you would. Oh! he was not the one to talk like that of poor Charlie. If Charlie was only Charlie, Raaf was nothing but Raaf—only a man who belonged to you, not one to admire independent of that. But whatever Raaf might do it would never have made any difference, certainly not to his mother, she did not suppose to any one, any more than it mattered to the poor old doctor what Charlie did, seeing he was his father's Charlie; and that nothing could change. She went along very slowly, thinking this to herself—not a very profound thought, but yet it filled her mind. The windows were already shining with firelight and lamplight, looking very bright. The drawing-room was not at all a large room. It was under the shade of a veranda and opened to the ground, which made it a better room for summer than for winter. Lucy woke up from her thoughts and wondered whether in the winter that was coming Mrs. Nugent would find it cold.

The two men went on round the common in the soft, damp evening air.

"That's one of the things one meets with, when one is long away," said Raaf, with a voice half confused in his beard and his cigar. "The old doctor was a landmark; fine old fellow, and knew a lot; never knew one like him for all the wild creatures—observing their ways, don't you know. He'd bring home as much from a walk as you or I would from a voyage—more, I daresay. I buy a few hideous things, and poor little Lucy shudders at them" (he was not so slow to notice as they supposed), "but I haven't got the head for much, while he—And all spoiled because of a fool of a boy not worth a thought."

"But his own, I suppose," said the other.

"Just that—his own—though why that should make such a difference. Now, Carry was worth a dozen of Charlie. Oh, I didn't speak very well of Carry just now!—true. She married a fellow not worth his salt, when, perhaps—But there's no answering for these things. Poor old doctor! There's scarcely anybody here except my mother that I couldn't have better spared."

"Let's hope it's a good thing for him," said Bertram, not knowing what to say.

"I can't think dying's better than living," said Raaf. "Oh, you mean—that? Well, perhaps; though it's hard to think of him," he said, with a sudden laugh, "in his old shiny coat with his brown gaiters in—what one calls—a better world. No kind of place suited him as well as here—he was so used to it. Somehow, though, on a quiet night like this, there's a kind of feeling, oh! I can't describe it in the least, as if—I say, you've been in many queer places, Bertram, and seen a lot?"

"That is true."

"Did you ever see anything that made you—feel any sort of certainty, don't you know? There's these stars, they say they're all worlds, globes, like this, and so forth. Who lives in them? That's what I've always wanted to know."

"Well, men like us can't live in them, for one thing, according to what the astronomers say."

"Men like us, ah! but then! We'll not be fellows like us when we're—the other thing, don't you know. There!" said Ralph; "I could have sworn that was the old man coming along to meet us; cut of his coat, gaiters and everything."

"You can't be well, old fellow, there is nobody."

"I know that as well as you," said Ralph, with a nervous laugh. "Do you think I meant I saw anything? Not such a fool; no, dear old man, I didn't see him; I wish I could, just to tell him one or two things about the beasts which he was keen about. I don't think that old fellow would be happy, Bertram, in a fluid, a sort of a place like a star, for instance, where there were no beasts."

"There's no reason to suppose they're fluid. And for that matter there may be beasts, as some people think; only I don't see, if you take in that, where you are to stop," said Bertram. "We are drawing it too fine, Wradisley, don't you think?"

"Perhaps we are, it's not my line of country. I wish you had known that old man. You're a fellow that makes out things, Bertram. He was quite comfortable—lots of books, and that museum which wasn't much of a museum, but he knew no better. Besides, there were a few good things in it. And enough of money to keep him all right. And then to think, Lord, that because of a fool of a fellow who was never out of hot water, always getting his father into hot water, never at peace, that good old man should go and break his heart, as they call it, and die."

"It may be very unreasonable, but it happens from time to time," Bertram said.

"By Jove, it is unreasonable! An old man that was really worth coming back to—and now he's clean swept away, and some baggage of a woman, probably no good, in his place, to turn Lucy's head, and perhaps bring us all to sixes and sevens, for anything I know."

"Why should you suppose so? There seems nothing but good in the lady, except that she is a stranger. So am I a stranger. You might as well believe that I should bring you to sixes and sevens. You're not well to-night, old fellow. You have got too much nonsense in your head."

"I suppose that's it—a touch of fever," said the other. "I'll take some quinine when I go home to-night." And with that wise resolution he drew up, having come back to the point from which they started, to wait for his sister at Mrs. Nugent's door.

CHAPTER III

The door of the little house was standing open when they drew up at the gate. It was a door at the side round the corner from the veranda, but with a porch which seemed to continue it. It was full of light from within, against which Lucy's figure stood dark. She was so much afraid to keep the gentlemen waiting that she had come out there to be ready, and was speaking her last words with her friend in the porch. Their voices sounded soft, almost musical, through the dusk and the fresh air; though, indeed, it was chiefly Lucy who was speaking. The men did not hear what she said, they even smiled a little, at least Bertram did, at the habit of the women who had always so much to say to each other about nothing; and who, though they had perhaps met before more than once that day, had still matter to murmur about down to the very last moment by the opening of the door. It went on indeed for two or three minutes while they stood there, notwithstanding that Lucy had cried, "Oh, there they are! I must go," at the first appearance of the tall shadows on the road. She was pleading with her friend to come up to the hall next day, which was the reason of the delay.

"Oh, Nelly, do come—to-morrow is an off day—they are not going to shoot. And I so want you to see Raaf; oh, I know he is not much to see—that's him, the tallest one. He has a huge beard. You'll perhaps think he's not very intellectual or that sort of thing; but he's our Raaf—he's mother's Raaf—and you're so fond of mother. And if I brought him to see you he would be shy and gauche. Do come, do come, to-morrow, Nelly; mother is so anxious you should come in good time."

Then the gentlemen, though they did not hear this, were aware of a new voice breaking in—a small, sweet treble, a child's voice—crying, "Me too, me too!"

"Yes, you too, Tiny; we always want you. Won't you come when Tiny wishes it, Nelly? You always give in to Tiny."

"Me come now," shouted Tiny, "see gemplemans; me come now."

Then there was a little scuffle and laughing commotion at the open door; the little voice loud, then others hushing it, and suddenly there came flying down the bank something white, a little fluttering line of whiteness upon the dark. The child flew with childish delight making its escape, while there was first a startled cry from the doorway, and then Lucy followed in pursuit. But the little thing, shouting and laughing, with the rush of infantile velocity, short-lived but swift, got to the bottom of the bank in a rush, and would have tripped herself up in her speed upon the fastening of the gate had not Bertram, coming a step forward, quickly caught her in his arms. There was not much light to see the child by—the little face like a flower; the waving hair and shining eyes. The little thing was full of laughter and delight in her small escapade. "Me see gemplemans, me see gemplemans," she said. Bertram lifted her up, holding her small waist firm in his two hands.

And then there came a change over Tiny. She became silent all at once, though without shrinking from the dark face up to which she was lifted. She did not twist in his grasp as children do, or struggle to be put down. She became quite still, drew a long breath, and fixed her eyes upon him, her little lips apart, her face intent. It was only the effect of a shyness which from time to time crept over Tiny, who was not usually shy; but it impressed the man very much who held her, himself quite silent for a moment, which seemed long to both, though it was scarcely appreciable in time, until Lucy reached the group, and with a cry of "Oh, Tiny, you naughty little girl!" restored man and child to the commonplace. Then the little girl wriggled down out of the stranger's grasp, and stole her hand into the more familiar one of Lucy. She kept her eyes, however, fixed upon her first captor.

"Oh, Tiny," cried Lucy, "what will the gentleman think of you—such a bold little girl—to run away from mamma, and get your death of cold, and give that kind gentleman the trouble of catching you. Oh, Tiny, Tiny!"

"Me go back to mummie now," Tiny said, turning her back upon them. It was unusual for this little thing, whom everybody petted, to be so subdued.

"You have both beards," cried Lucy, calling over her shoulder to her brother and his friend, as she led the child back. "She is frightened of you; but they are not bad gemplemans, Tiny, they are nice gemplemans. Oh, nurse, here she is, safe and sound."

"Me not frightened," Tiny said, and she turned round in the grip of the nurse, who had now seized upon her, and kissed her little hand. "Dood-night, gemplemans," Tiny cried. The little voice came shrill and clear through the night air, tinkling in the smallness of the sound, yet gracious as a princess; and the small incident was over. It was nothing at all; the simplest little incident in the world. And then Lucy took up her little strain, breathless with her rush, laughing and explaining.

"Tiny dearly loves a little escapade; she is the liveliest little thing! She has no other children to play with, and she is not afraid of anybody. She is always with her mother, you know, and hears us talk of everything."

"Very bad training for a child," said Ralph, "to hear all your scandal and gossip over your tea."

"Oh, Ralph, how common, how old fashioned you are!" cried Lucy, indignantly. "Do you think Mrs. Nugent talks scandal over her tea? or I—? I have been trying to make her promise to come up to lunch to-morrow, and then you shall see—that is, if she comes; for she was not at all sure whether she would come. She is not fond of strangers. She never will come to us when we have people—that is, not chance people—unless she knows them beforehand. Oh, you, of course, my brother, that's a different thing. I am sure I beg your pardon, Mr. Bertram, for making you wait, and for seeming to imply—and then Tiny rushing at you in that way."

"Tiny made a very sweet little episode in our walk," said Bertram. "Please don't apologize. I am fond of children, and the little thing gave me a look; children are strange creatures, they're only half of this world, I think. She looked—as if somehow she and I had met before."

"Have you, Mr. Bertram? did you perhaps know—her mother?" cried Lucy, in great surprise.

"It is very unlikely; I knew some Nugents once, but they were old people without any children, at least—No, I've been too long in the waste places of the earth ever to have rubbed shoulders with this baby; besides," he said, with a laugh, "if there was any recognition, it was she who recognized me."

"You are talking greater nonsense than I was doing, Bertram," said Ralph. "We're both out of sorts, I should think. These damp English nights take all the starch out of one. Come, let's get home. You shan't bring us out again after sunset, Lucy, I promise you that."

"Oh, sunset is not a bad time here," cried Lucy; "it's a beautiful time; it is only in your warm countries that it is bad. Besides, it's long after sunset; it's almost night and no moon for an hour yet. That's the chief thing I like going to town for, that it is never dark like this at night. I love the lamps—don't you, Mr. Bertram?—there is such company in them; even the cottage windows are nice, and that 'Red Lion'—one wishes that a public-house was not such a very bad thing, for it looks so ruddy and so warm. I don't wonder the men like it; I should myself, if—Oh, take care! there is a very wet corner there, just before you come to our gates. Why, there is some one coming out. Why—it's Reginald, Raaf!"

They were met, in the act of opening the gate, by Mr. Wradisley's slim, unmistakable figure. He had an equally slim umbrella, beautifully rolled up, in his hand, and walked as if the damp country road were covered with velvet.

"Oh, you are coming back," he said; "it's a fine night for a walk, don't you think so?—well, not after Africa, perhaps; but we are used in England to like these soft, grey skies and the feeling of—well, of dew and coolness in the air."

"I call it damp and mud," said Ralph, with an explosion of a laugh which seemed somehow to be an explosion manqué, as if the damp had got into that too.

"Ah," said his brother, reflectively. "Well it is rather a brutal way of judging, but perhaps you are right. I am going to take a giro round the common. We shall meet at dinner." And then he took off his hat to Lucy, and with a nod to Bertram went on. There was an involuntary pause among the three to watch him walking along the damp road—in which they had themselves encountered occasional puddles—as if a carpet had been spread underneath his dainty feet.

"Is this Rege's way?" said Ralph. "It's an odd thing for him surely—going out to walk now. He never would wet his feet any more than a cat. What is he doing out at night in the dark, a damp night, bad for his throat. Does my mother know?"

"Oh," said Lucy, with a curious confusion; "why shouldn't he go now, if he likes! It isn't cold, it's not so very damp, and Reginald's an Englishman, and isn't afraid of a bit of damp or a wet road. You are so hard to please. You are finding fault with everybody, Raaf."

"Am I?" he said. "Perhaps I am. I've grown a brute, being so much away."

"Oh, Raaf, I didn't mean that. Reginald has—his own ways. Don't you know, we never ask what he means, mother and I. He always means just what's the right thing, don't you know. It is a very nice time to—to take a giro; look how the sky's beginning to break there out of the clouds. I always like an evening walk; so did mother when she was strong enough. And then Reginald has such a feeling for art. He always says the village is so pretty with the lights in the windows, and the sweep of the fresh air on the common—and—and all that."

"Just so, Lucy," said Ralph.

She gave him a little anxious look, but she could not see the expression of his face in the darkness, any more than he could see what a wistful and wondering look was in her eyes. Bertram, looking on, formed his own conclusions, which were as little right as a stranger's conclusions upon a drama of family life suddenly brought before his eyes generally are. He thought that this correct and immaculate Mr. Wradisley had tastes known to his family, or at least to the ladies of his family, which were not so spotless as he appeared to be; or that there was something going on at this particular moment which contradicted the law of propriety and good order which was his nature. Was it a village amour? Was it some secret hanging over the house? There was a little agitation, he thought, in Lucy, and surprise in the brother, who was a stranger to all the ways of his own family, and evidently had a half-hostile feeling toward his elder. But the conversation became more easy as they went along, emerging from under the shadow of the trees and crossing the openings of the park. The great house came in sight as they went on, a solid mass amid all its surrounding of shrubbery and flower gardens, with the distance stretching clear on one side, and lights in many windows. It looked a centre of life and substantial, steadfast security, as if it might last out all the changes of fortune, and could never be affected by those vicissitudes which pull down one and set up another. Bertram could fancy that it had stood like a rock while many tempests swept the country. The individual might come and go, but this habitation was that of the race. And it was absurd to think that the little surprise of meeting its master on his way into the village late on an October evening, could have anything to do with the happiness of the family or its security. Bertram said to himself that his nerves were a little shaken to-night, he could not tell how. It was perhaps because of something visionary in this way of walking about an unknown place in the dark, and hearing of so many people like shadows moving in a world undiscovered. The old doctor, for example, whose image was so clear before his companion, that he could almost think he saw him, so clear that even to himself, a stranger, that old man had almost appeared; but more than anything else because of the child who, caught in her most sportive mood, had suddenly grown quiet in his arms, and given him that look, with eyes unknown, which he too could have sworn he knew. There were strange things in his own life that gave him cause to think. Was it not this that made him conscious of mystery and some disturbing influence in the family which he did not know, but which had received him as if he had been an absent brother too?

To see Mrs. Wradisley was, however, to send any thought of mystery or family trouble out of any one's mind. The lamps were lit in the drawing-room when they all went in, a little dazzled by the illumination, from the soft dark of the night. She was sitting where they had left her, in the warmth of the home atmosphere, so softly lighted, so quietly bright. Her white knitting lay on her knee. She had the evening paper in her hand, which had just come in; for it was one of the advantages of Wradisbury that, though so completely in the country, they were near enough to town to have an evening post. Mrs. Wradisley liked her evening paper. It was, it is true, not a late edition, perhaps in point of fact not much later than the Times of the morning—but she preferred it. It was her little private pleasure in the evening, when Lucy was perhaps out, or occupied with her friends, and Mr. Wradisley in his library. She nodded at them over her paper, with a smile, as they came in.

"I hope it is a fine night, and that you have had a pleasant walk, Mr. Bertram," she said.

"And is she coming, Lucy?"

"I could not get her to promise, mother," Lucy said.

"Oh, well, we must not press her. If she were not a little willful perhaps we should not like her so much," said Mrs. Wradisley, returning to her journal. And how warm it was! but not too warm. How light it was! but not too bright.

"Come and sit here, Raaf. I like to see you and make sure that you are there; but you need not talk to me unless you wish to," the mother said. She was not exacting. There was nothing wrong in the house, no anxiety nor alarm; nothing but family tranquility and peace.

CHAPTER IV

The little house called Greenbank was like a hundred other little houses in the country, the superior houses of the village, the homes of small people with small incomes, who still are ladies and gentlemen, the equals of those in the hall, not those in the cottage. The drawing-room was darkened in the winter days by the veranda, which was very desirable and pleasant in the summer, and chilled a little by the windows which opened to the floor on a level with the little terrace on which the house stood. It looked most comfortable and bright in the evening when the lamps were lighted and there was a good fire and the curtains were drawn. Mrs. Nugent was considered to have made a great difference in the house since the doctor's time. His heavy, old furniture was still in the dining-room, and indeed, more or less, throughout the rooms; but chintz or cretonne and appropriate draperies go a long way, according to the taste of the time. The new resident had been moderate and had not overdone it; she had not piled the stuffs and ornaments of Liberty into the old-fashioned house, but she had brightened the whole in a way which was less commonplace. Tiny was perhaps the great ornament of all—Tiny and indeed herself, a young woman not more than thirty, in the fulness of her best time, with a little dignity, which became her isolated position and her widowhood, and showed that, as the ladies in the neighborhood said, she was fully able to take care of herself. He would have been a bold man indeed who would have been rude or, what was more dangerous, overkind to Mrs. Nugent. She was one of those women, who, as it is common to say, keep people in their place. She was very gracious, very kind; but either she never forgot that she was alone and needed to be especially circumspect, or else it was her nature always to hold back a little, to be above impulse. I think this last was the case; for to be always on one's guard is painful, and betrays a suspicion of others or doubt of one's self, and neither of these was in Mrs. Nugent's mind. She liked society, and she did not shut herself out from the kind people who had adopted her, though she did not bring introductions or make any appeal to their kindness. There was no reason why she should shut them out; but she was not one who much frequented her neighbors' houses. She was always to be found in her own, with her little girl at her knee. Tiny was a little spoiled, perhaps, or so the ladies who had nurseries and many children to regulate, thought. She was only five, yet she sat up till eight, and had her bread-and-milk when her mother had her small dinner, at the little round table before the dining-room fire. Some of the ladies had even said to Mrs. Nugent that this was a self-indulgence on her part, and bad for the child; but, if so, she did not mind, but went on with the custom, which it was evident, for the moment did Tiny no harm.

The excitement of Tiny's escapade had been got over, and the child was sitting on the carpet in the firelight playing with her doll and singing to herself. She was always singing to herself or to the waxen companion in her arms, which was pale with much exposure to the heat of the fire. Tiny had a little tune which was quite different from the little snatches of song which she picked up from every one—from the butcher's boy and the postman and the maids in the kitchen, as well as from her mother's performances. The child was all ear, and sang everything, whatever she heard. But besides all this she had her own little tune, in which she kept singing sometimes the same words over and over again, sometimes her dialogues with her doll, sometimes scraps of what she heard from others, odds and ends of the conversation going on over her head. It was the prettiest domestic scene, the child sitting in front of the fire, in the light of the cheerful blaze, undressing her doll, hushing it in her arms, going through all the baby routine with which she was so familiar, singing, talking, cooing to the imaginary baby in her arms, while the pretty young mother sat at the side of the hearth, with the little table and work-basket overflowing with the fine muslin and bits of lace, making one of Tiny's pretty frocks or pinafores, which was her chief occupation. Sometimes Tiny's monologue was broken by a word from her mother; but sewing is a silent occupation when it is pursued by a woman alone, and generally Mrs. Nugent said nothing more than a word from time to time, while the child's little voice ran on. Was there something wanting to the little bright fireside—the man to come in from his work, the woman's husband, the child's father? But it was too small, too feminine a place for a man. One could not have said where he would sit, what he would do—there seemed no place for him, if such a man there had been.

Nevertheless a place was made for Mr. Wradisley when he came in, as he did immediately, announced by the smart little maid, carrying his hat in his hand. A chair was got for him out of the glow of the firelight, which affected his eyes. He made a little apology for coming so late.

"But I have a liking for the twilight; I love the park in the dusk; and as you have been so good as to let me in once or twice, and in the confidence that when I am intrusive you will send me away—"

"If you had come a little sooner," said Mrs. Nugent, in a frank, full voice, different from her low tones, "you might have taken care of Lucy, who ran in to see me."

"Lucy was well accompanied," said her brother; "besides, a walk is no walk unless one is alone; and the great pleasure of a conversation, if you will allow me to say so, is doubled when there are but two to talk. I know all Lucy's opinions, and she," he said, pausing with a smile, as if there was something ridiculous in the idea, "knows, or at least thinks she knows, mine."

"She knows more than she has generally credit for," said Mrs. Nugent; "but your brother was with her. It has pleased her so much to have him back."

"Raaf? yes. He has been so long away, it is like a stranger come to the house. He has forgotten the old shibboleths, and it takes one a little time to pick up his new ones. He is a man of the desert."

"Perhaps he has no shibboleths at all."

"Oh, don't believe that! I have always found the more unconventional a man is supposed to be, the furthest from our cut-and-dry systems, the more conventional he really is. We are preserved by the understood routine, and keep our independence underneath; but those who have to make new laws for themselves are pervaded by them. The new, uneasy code is on their very soul."

He spoke with a little warmth—unusual to him—almost excitement, his correct, calm tone quickening. Then he resumed his ordinary note.

"I hope," he said, with a keen look at her, "that poor Raaf made a favorable impression upon you."

Her head was bent over her needlework, which she had gone on with, not interrupting her occupation.

"I did not see him," she said. "Lucy ran in by herself; they waited for her, I believe, at the door."

"Me see gemplemans," sang Tiny, at his feet, making him start. She went on with her little song, repeating the words, "Dolly, such nice gemplemans. Give Dolly ride on's shoulder 'nother time."

And then Mrs. Nugent laughed, and told the story of Tiny's escapade. It jarred somehow on the visitor. He did not know what to make of Tiny; her little breaks into the conversation, the chant that could not be taken for remark or criticism, and yet was so, kept him in a continual fret; but he tried to smile.

"My brother," he said, "is the kind of primitive man who, I believe, pleases children—and dogs and primitive creatures generally—I—I beg your pardon, Mrs. Nugent."

"No; why should you?" She dropped her work on her knee and looked up at him with a laugh. "Tiny is quite a primitive creature. She likes what is kind and big and takes her up with firm hands. That is how I have always explained the pleasure infants take often in men. They are only accustomed to us women about them; but they almost invariably turn from us poor small things and rejoice in the hold of a man—when he's not frightened for them," she added, taking up her work again.

"As most men are, however," Mr. Wradisley said.

"Yes; that is our salvation. It would be too humiliating to think the little things preferred the look of a man. I have always thought it was the strength of his grasp."

"We shall shortly have to give in to the ladies even in that, they say," Mr. Wradisley went on, with relief in the changed subject. "Those tall girls—while we, it appears, are growing no taller, or perhaps dwindling—I am sure you, who are so womanly in everything, don't approve of that."

"Of tall girls? oh, why not? It is not their fault to be tall. It is very nice for them to be tall. I am delighted with my tall maid; she can reach things I have to get up on a chair for, and it is not dignified getting up on a chair. And she even snatches up Tiny before she has time to struggle or remonstrate."

"Tiny," said Mr. Wradisley, with a little wave of his hand, "is the be-all and end-all, I know; no one can hope to beguile your thoughts from that point."

Mrs. Nugent looked up at him quickly with surprise, holding her work suspended in her hand.

"Do you think it is quite right," he said, "or just to the rest of the world? A child is much, but still only a child; and here are you, a noble, perfect woman, with many greater capabilities. I do not flatter; you must know that you are not like other women—gossips, triflers, foolish persons—"

"Or even as this publican," said Mrs. Nugent, who had kept her eyes on him all the time, which had made him nervous, yet gave him a kind of inspiration. "I give alms of all I possess—I—Mr. Wradisley, do you really think this is the kind of argument which you would like a woman whom you profess to respect to adopt?"

"Oh, you twist what I say. I am conscious of the same thing myself, though I am, I hope, no Pharisee. To partly give up what was meant for mankind—will that please you better?—to a mere child—"

"You must not say such thing over Tiny's head, Mr. Wradisley. She understands a great deal. If she were not so intent upon this most elaborate part of Dolly's toilet for the night—"

"Mrs. Nugent, could not that spectator for one moment be removed?—could not I speak to you—if it were but for a minute—alone?"

She looked at him again, this time putting down the needle-work with a disturbed air.

"I wish to hear nothing, from any one, Mr. Wradisley, which she cannot hear."

"Not if I implored for one moment?"

His eyes, which were dull by nature, had become hot and shining, his colorless face was flushed; he was so reticent, so calm, that the swelling of something new within him took a form that was alarming. He turned round his hat in his hands as if it were some mystic implement of fate. She hesitated, and cast a glance round her at all the comfort of the little room, as if her shelter had suddenly been endangered, and the walls of her house were going to fall about her ears. Tiny all the time was very busy with her doll. She had arranged its nightgown, settled every button, tied every string, and now, holding it against her little bosom, singing to it, got up to put it to bed. "Mammy's darling," said Tiny, "everything as mammy has—dood dolly, dood dolly. Dolly go to bed."

Both the man and the woman sat watching her as she performed this little ceremony. Dolly's bed was on a sofa, carefully arranged with a cushion and coverlet. Tiny laid the doll down, listened, made as if she heard a little cry, bent over the mimic baby, soothing and quieting. Then she turned round to the spectators, holding up a little finger. "Gone to sleep," said Tiny in a whisper. "Hush, hush—dolly not well, not twite well—me go and ask nursie what she sinks."

The child went out on tip-toe, making urgent little gesticulations that the others might keep silence. There was a momentary hush; she had left the door ajar, but Mr. Wradisley did not think of that. He looked with a nervous glance at the doll on the sofa, which seemed to him like another child laid there to watch.

"Mrs. Nugent," he said at last, "you must know what I mean. I never thought this great moment of my life would come thus, as if it were a boy's secret, to be kept from a child!—but you know; I have tried to make it very clear. You are the only woman in the world—I want you to be my wife."

"Mr. Wradisley—God help me—I have tried to make another thing still more clear, that I can never more be any one's wife."

She clasped her hands and looked at him as if it were she who was the supplicant.

He, having delivered himself, became more calm; he regained his confidence in himself.

"I am very much in earnest," he said; "don't think it is lightly said. I have known since the first moment I saw you, but I have not yielded to any impulse. It has grown into my whole being; I accept Tiny and everything. I don't offer you any other inducements, for you are above them. You know a little what I am, but I will change my very nature to please you. Be my wife."

She rose up, the tears came in a flood to her eyes.

"Be content," she said; "it is impossible, it is impossible. Don't ask me any more, oh, for God's sake don't ask me any more, neither you nor any man. I would thank you if I could, but it is too dreadful. For the love of heaven, let this be final and go away."

"I cannot go away with such an answer. I have startled you, though I hoped not to do so. You are agitated, you have some false notions, as women have, of loving only once. Mrs. Nugent—"

She crossed the room precipitately in front of him as he approached toward her, and closing the door, stood holding it with her hand.

"I could explain in a word," she said, "but do not force me to explain—it would be too hard; it is impossible, only understand that. Here is my child coming back, who must not indeed hear this. I will give you my hand and say farewell, and you will never think of me again."

"That is the thing that is impossible," he said.

Tiny was singing at the door, beating against it. What an interruption for a tale—and such a love tale as his! Mr. Wradisley was terribly jarred in all his nerves. He was more vexed even than disappointed; he could not acknowledge himself disappointed. It was the child, the surprise, the shock of admitting for the first time such an idea; he would not believe it was anything else, not even when she held open the door for him with what in any other circumstances would have been an affront, sending him away. The child got between them somehow with her little song. "Dood-night, dood-night," said Tiny. "Come again anodder day," holding her mother's dress with one hand, and with the other waving to him her little farewell, as was her way.

He made a step or two across the little hall, and then came back. "Promise me that you will let this make no difference, that you will come to-morrow, that I shall see you again," he said.

"No, no; let it be over, let it be over!" she cried.

"You will come to-morrow? I will not speak to you if I must not; but make no difference. Promise that, and I will go away."

"I will come to-morrow," she said. "Good-by."

The maid was standing behind him to close the outer door. Did that account for the softening of her tone? or had she begun already to see that nothing was impossible—that her foolish, womanish prejudice about a dead husband could never stand in the way of a love like his? Mr. Wradisley's heart was beating in his ears, as he went down the bank, as it had never done before. He had come in great excitement, but it was with much greater excitement that he was going away. When the maid came running after him that laboring heart stood still for an instant. He thought he was recalled, and that everything was to be as he desired; he felt even a slight regret in the joy of being recalled so soon. It would have been even better had she taken longer to think of it. But it was only his umbrella which he had forgotten. Mr. Wradisley to forget his umbrella! That showed indeed the pass to which the man had come.

It was quite dark now, and the one or two rare passers-by that he met on the way passed him like ghosts, yet turned their heads toward him suspiciously, wondering who he was. They were villagers unwillingly out in the night upon business of their own; they divined a gentleman, though it was too dark to see him, and wondered who the soft-footed, slim figure could be, no one imagining for a moment who it really was. And yet he had already made two or three pilgrimages like this to visit the lady who for the first time in his life had made the sublime Mr. Wradisley a suitor. He felt, as he opened softly his own gate, that it was a thing that must not be repeated; but yet that it was in its way natural and seemly that his suit should not be precisely like that of an ordinary man. Henceforward it could be conducted in a different way, now that she was aware of his feelings without the cognizance of any other person. If it could be possible that her prejudices or caprice should hold out, nobody need be the wiser. But he did not believe that this would be the case. She had been startled, let it even be said shocked, to have discovered that she was loved, and by such a man as himself. There was even humility—the sweetest womanly quality—in her conviction that it was impossible, impossible that she, with no first love to give him, should be sought by him. But this would not stand the reflection of a propitious night, of a new day.

CHAPTER V

The dinner was quite a cheerful meal at Wradisbury that night. The master of the house was exactly as he always was. Punctilious in every kindness and politeness, perfect in his behavior. To see him take his mother in as he always did, as if she were the queen, and place her in her own chair, where she had presided at the head of that table for over forty years, was in itself a sight. He was the king regnant escorting a queen dowager—a queen mother, not exactly there by personal right, but by conscious delegation, yet supreme naturalness and reverence, from him. He liked to put her in her place. Except on occasions when there were guests he had always done it since the day of his father's death, with a sort of ceremony as showing how he gave her all honor though this supreme position was no longer her absolute due. He led her in with special tenderness to-night. It perhaps might not last long, this reign of hers. Another and a brighter figure was already chosen for that place, but as long as the mother was in it, the honor shown to her should be special, above even ordinary respect. I think Ralph was a little fretted by this show of reverence. Perhaps, with that subtle understanding of each other which people have in a family, even when they reach the extreme of personal difference or almost alienation, he knew what was in his brother's mind, and resented the consciousness of conferring honor which moved Reginald. In Ralph's house (or so he thought) the mother would rule without any show of derived power. It would be her own, not a grace conferred; but though he chafed he was silent, for it was very certain that there was not an exception to be taken, not a word to say. It is possible that Mrs. Wradisley was aware of it too, but she liked it, liked her son's magnanimous giving up to her of all the privileges which had for so long been hers. Many men would not have done that. They would have liked their houses to themselves; but Reginald had always been a model son. She was not in any way an exacting woman, and when she turned to her second son, come back in peace after so many wanderings, her heart overflowed with content. She was the only one in the party who was not aware that the master of the house had left his library in the darkening. The servants about the table all knew, and had formed a wonderfully close guess as to what was "up," as they said, and Lucy knew with a great commotion and trouble of her thoughts, wondering, not knowing if she were sorry or glad, looking very wistfully at her brother to see if he had been fortunate or otherwise. Was it possible that Nelly Nugent might be her sister, and sit in her mother's place? Oh, it would be delightful, it would be dreadful! For how would mamma take it to be dethroned? And then if Nelly would not, poor Reginald! Lucy watched him covertly, and could scarcely contain herself. Ralph and Mr. Bertram, I fear, did not think of Mrs. Nugent, but of something less creditable to Mr. Wradisley. The mother was the only one to whom any breach in his usual habits remained unknown.

"You really mean to have this garden party to-morrow, mother?" he said.

"Oh, yes, my dear, it is all arranged—the last, the very last of the season. Not so much a garden party as a sort of farewell to summer before your shooting parties arrive. We are so late this year. The harvest has been so late," Mrs. Wradisley said, turning toward Bertram. "St. Swithin, you know, was in full force this year, and some of the corn was still out when the month began. But the weather lately has been so fine. There was a little rain this morning, but still the weather has been quite remarkable. I am glad you came in time for our little gathering, for Raaf will see a number of old friends, and you, I hope, some of the nicest people about."

"I suspect I must have seen the nicest people already," said Bertram, with a laugh and a bow.

"Oh, that is a very kind thing to say, Mr. Bertram, and, indeed, I am very glad that Raaf's friend should like his people. But no, you will see some very superior people to-morrow. Lord Dulham was once a Cabinet Minister, and Colonel Knox has seen an immense deal of service in different parts of the world; not to speak of Mr. Sergeant—Geoffrey Sergeant, you know, who is so well known in the literary world—but I don't know whether you care for people who write," Mrs. Wradisley said.

"He writes himself," said Ralph, out of his beard. "Letters half a mile long, and leaders, and all sorts of things. If we don't look out he'll have us all in."

The other members of the party looked at Bertram with alarm. Mr. Wradisley with a certain half resentment, half disgust.

"Indeed," he said; "I thought I had been so fortunate as to discover for myself a most intelligent critic—but evidently I ought to have known."

"Don't say that," said Bertram, "indeed I'm not here on false pretenses. I'm not a literary man afloat on the world, or making notes. Only a humble newspaper correspondent, Mrs. Wradisley, and only that when it happens to suit me, as your son knows."

"Oh, I am sure we are very highly honored," said the lady, disturbed, "only Raaf, you should have told me, or I might have said something disagreeable about literary people, and that would have been so very—I assure you we are all quite proud of Mr. Sergeant, and still more, Mr. Bertram, to have some one to meet him whom he will—whom he is sure to—"

"You might have said he was a queer fish. I think he is," said Bertram, "but don't suppose he knows me, or any of my sort. Raaf is only playing you a trick. I wrote something about Africa, that's all. When one is knocking about the world for years without endless money to spend, anything to put a penny in one's purse is good. But I can't write a bit—except a report about Africa," he added, hurriedly.

"Oh, about Africa," Mrs. Wradisley said, with an expression of greater ease, and there was a little relief in the mind of the family generally. Bertram seized the opportunity to plunge into talk about Africa and the big game, drawing Ralph subtly into the conversation. It was not easy to get Ralph set a-going, but when he was so, there was found to be much in him wanting expression, and the stranger escaped under shelter of adventures naturally more interesting to the family than any he had to tell. He laughed a little to himself over it as the talk flowed on, and left him with not much pride in the literary profession, which he had in fact only played with, but which had inspired him at moments with a little content in what he did too. These good folk, who were intelligent enough, would have been a little afraid of him, not merely gratified by his acquaintance, had he been really a writer of books. They were much more at their ease to think him only a sportsman like Ralph, and a gentleman at large. When they went into the drawing-room afterwards, the conversation came back to the party of to-morrow, and to the pretty widow in the cottage, of whom Mrs. Wradisley began to talk, saying they would leave the flowers till Mrs. Nugent came, who was so great in decoration.

"I thought," said Ralph, "this widow of yours—was not to be here."

Mr. Wradisley interposed at this point from where he stood, with his back to the fire. "Ah," he said, "oh," with a clearing of his throat, "I happened to see Mrs. Nugent in the village to-day, and I certainly understood from her that she would be here."

"You saw her—after I did, Reginald?" said Lucy, in spite of herself.

"Now, how can you say anything so absurd, Lucy—when you saw her just before dinner, and Reginald could only have seen her in the morning, for he never goes out late," Mrs. Wradisley said.

Bertram felt that he was a conspirator. He gave a furtive glance at the others who knew different. He could see that Lucy grew scarlet, but not a word was said.

"You are mistaken, mother," said Mr. Wradisley, with his calm voice, "I sometimes do take a little giro in the evening."

"Oh, a giro;" said his mother, as if that altered the matter; "however," she added, "there never was any question about the party; that she fully knew we expected her for; but I wanted her to come for lunch that she might make Ralph's acquaintance before the crowd came; but it doesn't matter, for no doubt they'll meet often enough. Only when you men begin to shoot you're lost to all ordinary occupations; and so tired when you come in that you have not a word to throw at—a lady certainly, if you still may have at a dog."

"I am not so bent on meeting this widow, mother, as you seem to think," said Ralph.

"You need not always call her a widow. That's her misfortune; it's not her character," said Lucy, unconsciously epigrammatic.

"Oh, well, whatever you please—this beautiful lady—is that better? The other sounds designing, I allow."

"I think," said Mr. Wradisley, "that we have perhaps discussed Mrs. Nugent as much as is called for. She is a lady—for whom we all have the utmost respect." He spoke as if that closed the question, as indeed it generally did; and going across the room to what he knew was the most comfortable chair, possessed himself of the evening paper, and sitting down, began to read it. Mrs. Wradisley had by no means done with her evening paper, and that Reginald should thus take it up under her very eyes filled her soul with astonishment. She looked at him with a gasp, and then, after a moment, put out her hand for her knitting. Nothing that could have happened could have given her a more bewildering and mysterious shock.

All this, perhaps, was rather like a play to Bertram, who saw everything with a certain unconscious exercise of that literary faculty which he had just found so little impressive to the people among whom he found himself. They were very kind people, and had received him confidingly, asking no questions, not even wondering, as they might have done, what queer companion Ralph had picked up. Indeed, he was not at all like Ralph, though circumstances had made them close comrades. Perhaps if they could have read his life as he thought he could read theirs, they might not have opened their doors to him with such perfect trust. He had (had he?) the ruin of a woman's happiness on his heart, and the destruction of many hopes. He had been wandering about the world for a number of years, never knowing how to make up his mind on this question. Was it indeed his fault? Was it her fault? Were they both to blame? Perhaps the last was the truth; but he knew very well he would never get her, or any one, to confess or to believe that. There are some cases in which the woman has certainly the best of it; and when the man who has been the means of bringing a young, fair, blameless creature into great trouble, even if he never meant it, is hopelessly put in the wrong even when there may be something to be said for him. He was himself bewildered now and then when he thought it all over, wondering if indeed there might be something to be said for him. But if he could not even satisfy himself of that, how should he ever satisfy the world? He was a little stirred up and uncomfortable that night, he could scarcely tell why, for the brewing troubles of the Wradisleys, if it was trouble that was brewing, was unlikely to affect a stranger. Ralph, indeed, had been grumbling in his beard with complaints over what was in fact the blamelessness of his brother, but it did not trouble Bertram that his host should be too perfect a man. He had quite settled in his own mind what it was that was going to happen. The widow, no doubt, was some pretty adventuress who, by means of the mother and sister, had established a hold over the immaculate one, and meant to marry him and turn her patronesses adrift—the commonest story, vulgar, even. And the ladies would really have nothing to complain of, for Wradisley was certainly old enough to choose for himself, and might have married and turned off his mother to her jointure house years ago, and no harm done. It was not this that made Bertram sleepless and nervous, who really had so little to do with them, and no call to fight their battles. Perhaps it was the sensation of being in England, and within the rules of common life again, after long disruption from all ordinary circumstances of ordinary living. He to plunge into garden parties, and common encounters of men and women! He might meet some one who knew him, who would ask him questions, and attempt to piece his life together with guesses and conjectures. He had a great mind to repack his portmanteau and sling it over his shoulder, and tramp through the night to the nearest station. But to what good? For wherever he might go the same risk would meet him. How tranquil the night was as he looked out of the window, a great moon shining over the openings of the park, making the silence and the vacant spaces so doubly solitary! He dared not break the sanctity of that solitude by going out into it, any more than he dared disturb the quiet of the fully populated and deeply sleeping house. He had no right, for any caprice or personal cowardice of his, to disturb that stillness. And then it gave him a curious contradictory sensation, half of relief from his own thoughts, half of sympathy, to think that there were already here the elements of a far greater disturbance than any he could work, beginning to move within the house itself, working, perhaps, toward a catastrophe of its own. In the midst of all he suddenly stopped and laughed to himself, and went to bed at last with the most curiously subdued and softened sensation. He had remembered the look of the child whom he had lifted from the ground at the little gate of Greenbank—how she had suddenly been stilled in her childish mischief, and fixed him with her big, innocent, startled eyes. Poor little thing! She was innocent enough, whatever might be the nest from which she came. This was the thought with which he closed his eyes.

CHAPTER VI

Mr. Wradisley had never been known to give so much attention to any of his mother's entertainments before. Those which were more exclusively his own, the periodical dinners, the parties of guests occasionally assembled in the house either for political motives or in discharge of what he felt to be his duty as an important personage in the county, or for shooting—which was the least responsible of all, but still the man's part in a house of the highest class—he did give a certain solemn and serious attention to. But it had never been known that he had come out of himself, or even out of his library, which was in a manner the outer shell and husk of himself, for anything in the shape of an occasional entertainment, the lighter occurrences of hospitality. On this occasion, however, he was about all the morning with a slightly anxious look about his eyes, in the first place to see that the day promised well, to examine the horizon all round, and discuss the clouds with the head gardener, who was a man of much learning and an expert, as might be said, on the great question of the weather. That great authority gave it as his opinion that it would keep fine all day. "There may be showers in the evening, I should not wonder, but the weather will keep up for to-day," he said, backing his opinion with many minutiæ about the shape of the clouds and the indications of the wind. Mr. Wradisley repeated this at the breakfast table with much seriousness. "Stevenson says we may trust to having a fine day, though there may be showers in the evening," he said; "but that will matter less, mother, as all your guests will be gone by that time."

"Oh, Reginald, do you think Stevenson always knows?" cried Lucy, "He promised us fine weather the day of the bazaar, and there was a storm and everything spoiled in the afternoon."

"I am of the same opinion as Stevenson," said Mr. Wradisley, very quietly, which settled the matter; and, then, to be more wonderful still, he asked if the house were to be open, and if it was to be expected that any of the guests would wish to see his collection. "In that case I should direct Simmons to be in attendance," he said.

"Oh, if you would, Reginald!—that would give us great éclat," said his mother; "but I did not venture to ask. It is so very kind of you to think of it, of yourself. Of course it will be wished—everybody will wish it; but I generally put them off, you know, for I know you don't like to be worried, and I would not worry you for the world."

"You are too good to me, mother. There is no reason why I should be worried. It is, of course, my affair as much as any one's," he said, in his perfectly gentle yet pointed way, which made the others, even Mrs. Wradisley herself, feel a little small, as if she had been assuming an individual responsibility which she had not the right to assume.

"My show won't come to much if Rege is going to exhibit, mother," said Ralph. "I'd better keep them for another day."

"On the contrary," said Mr. Wradisley, with great suavity, "get out your savage stores. If the whole country is coming, as appears, there will be need for everything that we can do."

"There were just as many people last time, Reginald, but you wouldn't do anything," said Lucy, half aggrieved, notwithstanding her mother's "hush" and deprecating look.

"Circumstances are not always the same," her brother said; "and I understood from my mother that this was to be the last."

"For the season, Reginald," said Mrs. Wradisley, with a certain alarm in her tone.

"To be sure. I meant for the season, of course—and in the circumstances," he replied.

Mrs. Wradisley was not at all a nervous nor a timorous woman. She was very free of fancies, but still she was disturbed a little. She allowed Lucy to run on with exclamations and conjectures after the master of the house had retired. "What is the matter with Reginald? What has happened? What does he mean by it? He never paid any attention to our garden parties before."

Mrs. Wradisley was a very sensible woman, as has been said. After a very short interval she replied, calmly, "Most likely he does not mean anything at all, my dear. He has just taken a fancy to have everything very nice. It is delightful of him to let his collection be seen. That almost makes us independent of the weather, as there is so much in the house to see; but I do believe Stevenson is right, and that we are going to have a most beautiful day."

But though she made this statement, a little wonder remained in her mind. She had not, she remembered, been very well lately. Did Reginald think she was failing, and that it might really be his mother's last entertainment to her neighbors? It was not a very pleasant thought, for nothing had occurred for a long time to disturb the quiet tenor of Mrs. Wradisley's life, and Ralph had come back to her out of the wilds, and she was contented. She put the thought away, going out to the housekeeper to talk over anything that was necessary, but it gave her a little shock in spite of herself.

Mr. Wradisley, as may well be believed, had no thought at all of his mother's health, which he believed to be excellent, but he had begun to think a little of brighter possibilities, of the substitution of another feminine head to the house, and entertainments in which, through her, he would take a warmer interest. But it was only partly this, and partly nothing at all, as his sensible mother said, only the suppressed excitement in him and impulse to do something to get through the time until he should see Mrs. Nugent again and know his fate. He did not feel very much afraid, notwithstanding all she had said in the shock of the moment. He could understand that to a young widow, a fanciful young woman, more or less touched by the new fancies women had taken up, the idea of replacing her husband by another, of loving a second time, which all the sentimentalists are against, would be for the moment a great shock. She might feel the shock all the more if she felt, too, that there was something in her heart that answered to that alarming proposal, and might feel that to push off the thought with both hands, with all her might, was the only thing possible. But the reflections of the night and of the new morning, which had risen with such splendor of autumnal sunshine, would, he felt almost sure, make a great difference. Mrs. Nugent did not wear mourning; it was probably some years since her husband's death. She was not very well off, and did not seem to have many relations who could help her, or she would not have come here so unfriended, to a district in which nobody knew her. Was it likely that she should resist all that he had to offer, the love of a good man, the shelter of a well-known, wealthy, important name and house? It was not possible that for a mere sentiment a woman so full of sense as she was, could resist these. The love of a good man—if he had not had a penny in the world, that would be worth any woman's while; and she would feel that. He thought, as he arranged with a zeal he had never felt before, the means of amusing and occupying his mother's guests, that he would have all the more chance of getting her by herself, of finding time and opportunity to lead her out of the crowd to get her answer. Surely, surely, the chances were all in favor of a favorable answer. It was not as if he were a nobody, a chance-comer, a trifling or unimportant person. He had always been aware that he was an important person, and it seemed impossible that she should not see it too.

Ralph Wradisley and his friend Bertram went out for a long walk. They were both "out of it," the son as much as the visitor, and both moved with similar inclinations to run away. "Of course I'll meet some fellows I know," Ralph said. "Shall I though? The fellows of my age are knocking about somewhere, or married and settled, and that sort of thing. I'll meet the women of them, sisters, and so forth, and perhaps some wives. It's only the women that are fixtures in a country like this; and what are the women to you and me?"

"Well, to me nothing but strangers—but so would the men be too."

"Ah, it's all very well to talk," said Ralph. "Women have their place in society, and so forth—wouldn't be so comfortable without them, I suppose. But between you and me, Bertram, there ain't very much in women for fellows like us. I'm not a marrying man—neither are you, I suppose? The most of them about here are even past the pretty girl stage, don't you know, and I don't know how to talk to them. Africa plays the deuce with you for that."

"No," said Bertram, "I am not a marrying man. I am—I feel I ought to tell you, Wradisley—there never was any need to go into such questions before, and you may believe I don't want to carry a placard round my neck in the circumstances;—well—I am a married man, and that is the truth."

Ralph turned upon him with a long whistle and a lifting of the eyebrows. "By Jove!" he said.

"I hope you won't bear me a grudge for not telling you before. In that case I'll be off at once and bother you no more."

"Stuff!" cried Ralph; "what difference can it make to me? I have thought you had something on your mind sometimes; but married or single, we're the same two fellows that have walked the desert together, and helped each other through many a scrape. I'm sorry for you, old chap—that is, if there's anything to be sorry for. Of course, I don't know."

"I've been afloat on the world ever since," said Bertram. "It was all my fault. I was a cursed fool, and trapped when I was a boy. Then I thought the woman was dead—had all the proofs and everything, and—You say you know nothing about that sort of thing, Wradisley. Well, I won't say anything about it. I fell in love with a lady every way better than I—she was—perhaps you do know more than you say. I married her—that's the short and the long of it; and in a year, when the baby had come, the other woman, the horrible creature, arrived at my very door."

"Good Lord!" cried Ralph softly, in his beard.

"She was dying, that was one good thing; she died—in my house. And then—We were married again, my wife and I—she allowed that; but—I have never seen her since," said Bertram, turning his head away.

"By Jove!" said Ralph Wradisley once more, in his beard; and they walked on in silence for a mile, and said not another word. At last—

"Old chap," said Ralph, touching his friend on the shoulder, "I never was one to talk; but it's very hard lines on you, and Mrs. Bertram ought to be told so, if she were the queen."

Bertram shook his head. "I don't know why I told you," he said; "don't let us talk of it any more. The thing's done and can't be undone. I don't know if I wish any change. When two paths part in this world, Wradisley, don't you know, the longer they go, the wider apart they get—or at least that's my experience. They say your whole body changes every seven years—it doesn't take so long as that to alter a man's thoughts and his soul—and a woman's, too, I suppose. She's far enough from me now, and I from her. I'm not sure I—regret it. In some ways it—didn't suit me, so to speak. Perhaps things are best as they are."

"Well," said Ralph, "I'd choose a free life for myself, but not exactly in that way, Bertram—not if I were you."

"Fortunately we are none of us each other," Bertram said, with a laugh which had little mirth in it. He added, after a moment: "You'll use your own discretion about telling this sorry tale of mine, Wradisley. I felt I had to tell you. I can't go about under false pretenses while you're responsible for me. Now you know the whole business, and we need not speak of it any more."

"All right, old fellow," Ralph said; and they quickened their pace, and put on I don't know how many miles more before they got back—too late for lunch, and very muddy about the legs—to eat a great deal of cold beef at the sideboard, while the servants chafed behind them, intent upon changing the great dining-room into a bower of chrysanthemums and temple of tea. They had to change their dress afterwards, which took up all their time until the roll of carriages began. Bertram, for his part, being a stranger and not at all on duty, took a long time to put himself into more presentable clothes. He did not want to have any more of the garden party than was necessary. And his mind had been considerably stirred up by his confession, brief as it was. It had been necessary to do it, and his mind was relieved; but he did not feel that it was possible to remain long at Wradisbury now that he had disclosed his mystery, such as it was. What did they care about his mystery? Nothing—not enough to make a day's conversation out of it. He knew very well in what way Ralph would tell his story. He would not announce it as a discovery—it would drop from his beard like the most casual statement of fact: "Unlucky beggar, Bertram—got a wife and all that sort of thing—place down Devonshire way—but he and she don't hit it off, somehow." In such terms the story would be told, without any mystery at all. But Bertram, who was a proud man, did not feel that he could live among a set of people who looked at him curiously across the table and wondered how it was that he did not "hit it off" with his wife. He knew that he would read that question in Mrs. Wradisley's face when she bade him good-morning; and in Lucy's eyes—Lucy's eyes, he thought, with a half smile, would be the most inquisitive—they would ask him a hundred questions. They would say, with almost a look of anxiety in them, "Oh! Mr. Bertram—why?" It amused him to think that Lucy would be the most curious of them all, though why, I could not venture to say. He got himself ready very slowly, looking out from the corner of his window at all the smart people of the county gathering upon the lawn. There was tennis going on somewhere, he could hear, and the less loud but equally characteristic stroke of the croquet balls. And the band, which was a famous band from London, had begun to play. If he was to appear at all, it was time that he should go downstairs; but, as a matter of fact, he was not really moved to do this, until he saw a little flight across the green of a small child in white, so swift that some one had to stoop and pick her up as he picked up Tiny at the gate of Greenbank. The man on the lawn who caught this little thing lifted her up as Bertram had done. Would the child be hushed by his grasp, and look into his face as Tiny had looked at him? Perhaps this was not Tiny—at all events, it gave no look, but wriggled and struggled out of its captor's hands. This sight decided Bertram to present himself in the midst of Mrs. Wradisley's guests. He wanted to see Tiny once again.


CHAPTER VII

Bertram soon lost himself among the crowd on the lawn, among all the county people and the village people, making his way out and in, in a solitude which never feels so great as among a crowd. It seemed wonderful to him, as it is specially to those who have been more or less in what is called "Society," that he saw nobody whom he knew. That is a thing almost impossible to happen for those that are born within that charmed circle. Whether at the end of the world or in the midst of it, it is incredible that you should see an assemblage of human creatures without discovering one who is familiar at least, if not friendly—unless, indeed, you wander into regions unknown to society; and Mrs. Wradisley and her guests would all have been indignant indeed had that been for a moment imagined of them. But yet this is a thing that does happen now and then, and Bertram traversed the lawns and flower gardens and conservatories without meeting a single face which he recognized or being greeted by one voice he had ever heard before. To be sure, this was partly owing to the fact that the person of whom he was specially in search was a very small person, to be distinguished at a very low pitch of stature near to the ground, not at tall on a level with the other forms. There were a few children among the groups on the lawn, and he pursued a white frock in various directions, which, when found, proved to contain some one who was not Tiny; but at last he came to that little person clinging to Lucy's skirts as she moved about among her mother's guests. Lucy turned round upon Bertram with a little surprise to find him so near her, and then a little rising glow of color and a look in her mild eyes of mingled curiosity and compassion, which penetrated him with sudden consciousness, annoyance, yet amusement. Already it was evident Ralph had found a moment a tell his tale. "Oh, Mr. Bertram!" Lucy said. She would have said precisely the same in whatever circumstances; the whole difference was in the tone.

Then a small voice was uplifted at her feet. "It is the gemplemans," Tiny said.

"So you remember me, little one? though we only saw each other in the dark. Will you come for a walk with me, Tiny?" Bertram said.

The child looked at him with serious eyes. Now that he saw her in daylight she was not the common model of the angelic child, but dark, with a little olive tint in her cheeks and dark brown hair waving upon her shoulders. He scarcely recognized, except by the serious look, the little runaway of the previous night, yet recognized something in her for which he was not at all prepared, which he could not explain to himself. Why did the child look at him so? And he looked at her, not with the half fantastic, amused liking which had made him seek her out, but seriously too, infected by her survey of him, which was so penetrating and so grave. After Tiny had given him this investigating look, she put her little velvety hand into his, with the absolute confidence of her age, "'Ess, me go for a walk," she said.

"Now, Tiny, talk properly to this gentleman; let him see what a lady you can be when you please," said Lucy. "She's too old to talk like that, isn't she, Mr. Bertram? She is nearly five! and she really can talk just as well as I can, when she likes. Tiny! now remember!" Lucy was very earnest in her desire that Tiny should do herself justice; but once more lifted the swift, interrogative look which seemed to say, as he knew she would, "Oh, Mr. Bertram—why?"

"Where shall we go for our walk, Tiny?" Bertram said.

"Take Tiny down to the pond; nobody never take me down to the wasser. Mamma says Tiny tumble in, but gemplemans twite safe. Come, come, afore mummie sees and says no."

"But, Tiny, if you're sure your mother would say no—"

"Qwick, qwick!" cried Tiny. "If mummie says nuffin, no matter; but if she says no!"—this was uttered with a little stamp of the foot and raised voice as if in imitation of a familiar prohibition—"then Tiny tan't go. Come along, quick, quick."

It was clear that Tiny's obedience was to the letter, not the spirit.

"But I don't know the way," said Bertram, holding a little back.

"Come, come!" cried the child, dragging him on. "Tiny show you the way."

"And what if we both fall in, Tiny?"

"You's too old, too big gemplemans to fall into the wasser—too big to have any mummie."

"Alas! that's true," he said.

"Then never mind," said the little girl. "No mummie, no nursie, nobody to scold you. You can go in the boat if you like. Come! Oh, Tiny do, do want to go in the boat; and there's flowers on the udder side, fordet-me-nots!—wants to get fordet-me-nots. Come, gemplemans, come!"

"Would you like to ride on my shoulder? and then we shall go quicker," he said.

She stood still at once, and held out her arms to be lifted up. Now Bertram was not the kind of man who makes himself into the horse, the bear, the lion, as occasion demands, for the amusement of children. He was more surprised to find himself with this little creature seated on his shoulder, than she was on her elevated seat, where indeed she was entirely at her ease, guiding him with imperative tugs at the collar of his coat and beating her small foot against his breast, as if she had the most perfect right to his attention and devotion. "This way, this way," sang Tiny; "that way nasty way, down among the thorns—this way nice way; get fordet-me-nots for mummie; mummie never say nuffin—Tiny tan go!"

He found himself thus hurrying over the park, with the child's voice singing its little monologue over his head, flushed with rebellion against the unconscious mother, much amused at himself. And yet it was not amusement; it was a curious sensation which Bertram could not understand. It is not quite an unexampled thing to fall in love with a child at first sight; but he was not aware that he had ever done it before, and to be turned so completely by the child into the instrument of her little rebellions and pleasures was more wonderful still. He laughed within himself, but his laugh went out of him like the flame of a candle in the wind. He felt more like to cry, if he had been a subject for crying. But why he could not tell. Never was man in a more disturbed and perplexed state of mind. Guided by Tiny's pullings and beatings, he got to the pond at last, a pond upon the other side of which there was, strange to say, visible among the russet foliage, one little clump of belated forget-me-nots quite out of season. The child's quick eye had noted them as she had gone by with her nurse on some recent walk. Bertram knew a great many things, but it is very doubtful whether he was aware that it was wonderful to find forget-me-nots so late. And Tiny was a sight to see when he put her down in the stern of the boat and pulled across the pond with a few long strokes. Her eyes, which had a golden light in their darkness, shone with triumph and delight; the brown of her little sunburnt face glowed transparent as if there was a light within; her dark curls waved; the piquancy of the complexion so unusual in a child, the chant of her little voice shouting, "Fordet-me-nots, fordet-me-nots!" her little rapture of eagerness and pleasure carried him altogether out of himself. He had loved that complexion in his day; perhaps it was some recollection, some resemblance, which was at the bottom of this strange absorption in the little creature of whose very existence he had not been aware till last night. Now, if he had been called on to give his very life for Tiny he would have been capable of it, without knowing why; and, indeed, there would have been a very likely occasion of giving his life for Tiny, or of sacrificing hers, as her mother foresaw, if he had not caught her as she stretched herself out of the boat to reach the flowers. His grip of her was almost violent—and there was a moment during which Tiny's little glow disappeared in a sudden thunder-cloud, changing the character of her little face, and a small incipient stamp of passion on the planks betrayed rebellion ready to rise. But Tiny looked at Bertram, who held her very firmly, fixed him with much the same look as she had given him at their first meeting, and suddenly changed countenance again. What did that look mean? He had said laughingly on the previous night that it was a look of recognition. She suddenly put her two little hands round his neck, and said, "Tiny will be dood." And the effect of the little rebel's embrace was that tears—actual wet tears, which for a moment blinded eyes which had looked every kind of wonder and terror in the face—surprised him before he knew. What did it mean? What did it mean? It was too wonderful for words.

The flowers were gathered after this in perfect safety and harmony; Tiny puddling with her hands in the mud to get the nearest ones "nice and long," as she said, while Bertram secured those that were further off. And then there arose a great difficulty as to how to carry these wet and rather muddy spoils. Tiny's pretty frock, which she held out in both hands to receive them like a ballet dancer, could not be thought of.

"For what would your mother say if your frock was wet and dirty?" said Bertram, seriously troubled.

"Mummie say, 'Oh, Tiny, Tiny, naughty schild,'" said the little girl, with a very grave face; "never come no more to garden party."

Finally an expedient was devised in the shape of Bertram's handkerchief tied together at the corners, and swung upon a switch of willow which was light enough for Tiny to carry; in which guise the pair set out again toward the house and the smart people, Tiny once more on Bertram's shoulder, with the bundle of flowers bobbing in front of his nose, and, it need not be said, some trace of the gathering of the flowers and of the muddy edges of the pool, and the moss-grown planks of the boat showing on both performers—on Tiny's frock, which was a little wet, and on Bertram's coat, marked by the beating of the little feet, which had gathered a little mud and greenness too. Tiny began to question him on the returning way.

"Gemplemans too big to have got a mummie," said Tiny; "have you got a little girl?"

Not getting any immediate answer to this question, she sang it over him in her way, repeating it again and again—"Have zoo dot a little girl?"—her dialect varying according to her caprice, until the small refrain got into his head.

The man was utterly confused and troubled; he could not give Tiny any answer, nor could he answer the wonderful maze of questions and thoughts which this innocent demand of hers awakened in his breast. When they came within sight of the lawn and its gay crowd, Bertram bethought him that it would be better to put his little rider down, and to present her to perhaps an anxious or angry mother on a level, which would make her impaired toilet less conspicuous. After all, there was nothing so wonderful in the fact that a little girl had dirtied her frock. He had no occasion to feel so guilty and disturbed about it. And this is how it happened that the adventurers appeared quite humbly, Tiny not half pleased to descend from her eminence and carrying now over her shoulder, as Bertram suggested, the stick which supported her packet of flowers, while he walked rather shamefaced by her, holding her hand, and looking out with a little trepidation for the mother, who, after all, could not bring down very condign punishment upon him for running away with her child.

CHAPTER VIII

Mrs. Nugent had been very unwilling to fulfill her promise and appear at Mrs. Wradisley's party. She had put off her arrival till the last moment, and as she walked up from the village with her little girl she had flattered herself that, arriving late under shelter of various other parties who made much more commotion, she might have escaped observation. But if Bertram, of whom she knew nothing, had been intent on finding Tiny, Mr. Wradisley was much more intent on finding Tiny's mother. He had been on the watch and had not missed her from the first moment of her appearance, carefully as she thought she had sheltered it from observation. And even her appearance, though she had condemned it herself as excited and sullen, when she gave herself a last look in the glass before coming away, did not discourage him. Excitement brightens a woman's eye and gives additional color to her face, or at least it did so to Nelly. The gentle carelessness of the ordinary was not in her aspect at all. She was more erect, carrying her animated head high. Nobody could call her ordinary at any time. She was so full of life and action. But on that day every line of her soft, light dress seemed to have expression. The little curls on her forehead were more crisp, the shining of her eyes more brilliant. There was a little nervous movement about her mouth which testified to the agitation in her. "Is there anything wrong, dear?" asked Mrs. Wradisley, pausing, holding her by the hand, looking into her face, startled by this unusual look, even in the midst of her guests.

"Oh, no—yes. I have had some disturbing news, but nothing to take any notice of. I will tell you afterwards," Mrs. Nugent said. Lucy too hung upon her, eager to know what was the matter. "Only some blunders—about my affairs," she had replied, "which I can set right."

"Oh, if that is all!" Lucy had cried, running off to salute some other new-comers and carrying Tiny in her train. "Affairs" meant business to Lucy, and business, so far as she was aware, touched only the outside, and could have nothing to do with any one's happiness. Besides, her mind was in a turmoil for the moment with that strange story of Mrs. Bertram which her mother had just told her by way of precaution, filtered from Ralph. "Mr. Bertram is married, it appears; but he and his wife don't get on," was what Mr. Wradisley had said. Lucy's imagination had, as we are aware, been busy about Bertram, and she was startled by this strange and sudden conclusion to her self-inquiry whether by any chance he might be the Ideal man.

It was thus that Mrs. Nugent had been suddenly left without even the protection of her child, and though she had managed for some time to hide herself, as she supposed (though his watchful gaze in reality followed her everywhere), from her host amid the crowd of other people assembled, there came the inevitable moment when she could keep herself from him no longer. He came up to her while the people who surrounded dispersed to examine his collection or to go in for tea.

"But I have seen your collection, Mr. Wradisley," she said; "you were so kind as to show me everything."

"It is not my collection," he said; "it is—a flower I want to show you. The new orchid—the new—Let me take you into the conservatory. I must," he said, in a lower tone. "You must be merciful and let me speak to you."

"Mr. Wradisley," she cried, almost under her breath, "do not, for pity's sake, say any more."

"I must," he said, impetuously. "I must know." And then he added in his usual tone, "Stevenson is very proud of it. It is a very rare kind, you know, and the finest specimen, he says."

"Oh, what is that, Mr. Wradisley?—an orchid? May I come too?" said another guest, without discrimination.

"Certainly," he said; "but all in its order. Simmons comes first, Stevenson afterwards. You have not seen my Etruscan collection." Mrs. Nugent was aware that he had caught a floating ribbon of the light cloak she carried on her arm, and held it fast while he directed with his usual grave propriety the other lady by her side. "Now," he said, looking up to her. If it was the only thing that could be done, then perhaps it was better that it should be done at once. He led her through the lines of gleaming glass, the fruit, and the flowers, for Wradisbury was famous for its vineries and its conservatories—meeting a few wanderers by the way, whom it was difficult to prevent from following—till at last they got to the inner sanctuary of all, where a great fantastic blossom, a flower, but counterfeiting something that was not a flower, blazed aloft in the ruddy afternoon light, which of itself could never have produced that unnatural tropical blossom. Neither the man nor the woman looked at the orchid. She said to him eagerly before he could speak: "This is all dreadful to me. You ought to let me go. You ought to be satisfied with my word. Should I speak as I have done if I had not meant it? Mr. Wradisley, for God's sake, accept what I have already said to you and let me go."

"No," he said. She stood beside the flower, her brown beauty shining against the long leaves and strong stem of the beautiful monster, and he planted himself in front of her as if to prevent her escape. "You think I am tyrannical," he said; "so I am. You are shocked and startled by what I have said to you. It is because I understand that that I am so pressing, so arbitrary now. Mrs. Nugent, you can't bear that a man should speak to you of love. You think that love only comes once, that your heart should be buried with your husband; that is folly, it is fancy, it is prejudice, it is not a real feeling. That is why I force you almost to hear me. Pause a moment, and hear me."

"Not a moment, not a moment!" she cried. "It is more than that. Take my word for it, and let me go and say no more."

"A widow," he said, "you make up an idea to yourself that it's something sacred. You are never to love, never to think of any one again. But all that is fiction—don't interrupt me—it is mere fiction. You are living, and he is dead."

"You force me," she cried, "to betray myself. You force me—to tell you my secrets. You have no right to force my secret from me. Mr. Wradisley, every word you say to me is an offense. It is my own fault; but a man ought surely to be generous and take a woman's word without compelling her in self defense—"

"I know by heart all that you can say in self-defense," he cried, vehemently, "and you ought to be told that these are all fictions—sentimentalisms—never to be weighed against a true affection—a man's love—and home and protection—both for yourself and your child."

The young woman's high spirit was aroused. "I will have no more of this," she said. "I am quite able to protect myself and my child. Let me go—I will go, Mr. Wradisley. I do not call this love. I call it persecution. Not a word more."

Mr. Wradisley was more astonished than words could say. He fell back, and allowed her to pass. He had thought, with a high hand, in the exercise of that superior position and judgment which everybody allowed him, to bring her to reason. Was it possible that she was not to be brought to reason? "I think," he said, "Mrs. Nugent, that when you are calm and consider everything at your leisure you will feel—that I am justified."

"You can never be justified in assuming that you know—another person's position and feelings; which you don't, and can't know."

"I argue from the general," said Mr. Wradisley, with an air almost of meekness, "and when you think—when you take time to consider—"

"No time would make any difference," she said, quickly; and then, for she was now free and going back again toward the lawn, her heart smote her. "Don't bear me any malice," she said. "I respect you very much; any woman might be proud—of your love"—her face gave a little twitch, whether toward laughing or crying it was difficult to tell—"but I couldn't have given you mine in any circumstances, not if I had been—entirely free."

"Which you are—from everything but false sentiment," he said, doggedly.

But what did it matter?—he was following her out, her face was turned from him, her ears were deaf to his impressive words, as her eyes were turned from his looks, which were more impressive still. Mr. Wradisley had failed, and it was the first time for many years that he had done so; he had even forgotten that such a thing was possible. When they came, thus walking solemnly one behind the other, to the outer house where some of the other guests were lingering, Mrs. Nugent stopped to speak to some of them, to describe the new orchid. "It is the most uncanny thing I ever saw," she said. And then Lady Dulham, the great lady of that side of the county, the person whom he most disliked, appealed to Mr. Wradisley to show her too the new wonder. It was perhaps on the whole the best way he could have got out of this false position. He offered the old lady his arm with a deeply wounded, hotly offended heart.

Mrs. Nugent lingered a little with the others in the great relief and ease of mind which, though it was only momentary, was great. She had not after all been obliged to reveal any of her secrets, whatever they might be. If he had been less peremptory, more reasonable, she would have been obliged to explain to him; and that she had very little mind to do. After the first relief, however, she began to feel what a blow had been struck at her temporary comfort in this place by so untoward an accident. His mother and sister were her chief friends; they had received her so generously, so kindly, with such confidence. Her secret was no guilty one, but still it had made her uncomfortable, it had been the subject of various annoyances; but none of these kind people had asked her any questions; they had received her for herself, never doubting. And now it seemed that she had only appeared among them to do harm. She was a pretty and attractive young woman, and not altogether unaware that people liked her on that account; but yet she never had been one of those women with whom everybody is acquainted, in novels, at least, before whom every man falls down. She had had her share, but she had not been persecuted by inopportune lovers. And she had not entertained any alarm in respect to Mr. Wradisley. She hoped now that his pride would help him through it, and that nobody would be the wiser; but still she could not continue here under the very wing of the family after so humiliating its head, either meeting him, or compelling him to avoid her. She went on turning over this question in her mind, pausing to talk to this one and that one, to do her duty to Mrs. Wradisley still by amusing and occupying her guests, putting on her smiles as if they had been ribbons to conceal some little spot or rent beneath. Indeed, it was no rent. She had not been very long at Wradisbury. It would be no dreadful business to go away. She was neither without friends nor protectors, and London was always a ready and natural refuge, where it would be so simple to go. But this fiasco, as she called it to herself, vexed her. She wanted to get away as soon as possible, to think it over at leisure, to find Tiny, who no doubt was hanging on Lucy Wradisley's skirts somewhere, or else playing with the other children, and to steal home as soon as there was any pretext for departure. She felt that she would prefer not to meet his mother's eye.

She was beginning to get very impatient of waiting when at last she caught sight of Tiny being set down on the ground from somebody's shoulders. She did not pay any attention for the moment to the man. Tiny had so many friends; for the child was not shy; she had no objection to trust herself to any one who pleased her, though it was not every one who had this advantage and pleased Tiny. The mother saw at once that Tiny's best frock had suffered, and a momentary alarm about the pond, which was one of her favorite panics, seized her. But the child was evidently quite right, which settled that question. She went to meet Tiny with a word of playful reproof for her disheveled condition on her lips. The child and her guardian were coming round a clump of trees which hid them for a moment, and toward which Mrs. Nugent turned her steps. She heard the small voice running on in its usual little sing-song of monologue.

"Have zoo dot a little girl? Have zoo dot a little girl?"

What an odd question for Tiny to ask! The child must really be trained to be a little more like other children, not to push her little inquiries so far, not to ask questions. Mrs. Nugent could not help smiling a little at the sound of her small daughter's voice, especially as there was no reply made to it. The man had a big beard, that was all she had observed of him; perhaps it was the other son, the brother Raaf, the adventurer, or perhaps prodigal, who had newly come home.

These were her thoughts as she turned round the great bole of that big tree of which the Wradisleys were so proud. Bertram was coming on the other side, half smiling, too, at Tiny's little song; while she, spying some children in the distance, swayed backward from his hold to call to them, and then detaching herself from his hand altogether, ran back a few paces to show them her treasures. His face half averted for a moment looking after her thus, gave Mrs. Nugent one breath of preparation, but none to him, who turned round again half conscious of some one coming to meet him, with still that half smile and the tender expression in his eyes. He stood still, he wavered for a moment as if, strong man as he was, he would have fallen.

"My God—Nelly!" he cried.

CHAPTER IX

After the most successful party, even if it is only a garden party, a flatness is apt to fall upon the family of the entertainers who have been so nobly doing their best to amuse their friends. Besides the grateful sense of success, and of the fact that the trouble is well over, comes a flagging of both physical and mental powers. The dinner at Wradisbury was heavy after the great success of the afternoon; there was a little conversation about that, and about how everybody looked, and on Ralph's part, who was decidedly the least dull of the party, on the changes that time had made, especially upon the women whom he remembered as little girls, and who were now, as he said, "elderly," some of them with little girls of their own; but neither Mr. Wradisley nor Mr. Bertram were at all amused, and Lucy was tired, and agreeing with Ralph completely in his estimation of the old young ladies, was not exhilarated by it as she might have been. The master of the house did not indeed betray fatigue or ill-humor, he was too well bred for that. But he was a little cross to the butler, and dissatisfied with the dinner, which was an unusual thing; he even said something to his mother about "your cook," as if he thought the sins of that important person resulted from the fact that she was Mrs. Wradisley's cook, and had received bad advice from her mistress. When he was pleased he said "my cook," and on ordinary occasions "the cook," impersonally and impartially. Bertram on the other hand, had the air of a man who had fallen from a great height, and had not been able to pick himself up—he was pale, his face was drawn. He scarcely heard when he was spoken to. When he perceived that he was being addressed he woke up with an effort. All this Lucy perceived keenly and put down to what was in fact its real reason, though with a difference. She said to herself:

"Nelly Nugent must have known him. She must have known his wife and all about him, and how it was they didn't get on. I'll make her tell me," Lucy said to herself, and she addressed herself very particularly to Mr. Bertram's solace and entertainment, partly because she was romantically interested and very sorry for him, and partly to show her mother, who had told her with a certain air that Mr. Bertram was married, that his marriage made not the slightest difference to her. She tried to draw him out about Tiny, who was the first and most natural subject.

"Isn't she a delightful little thing? I am sure she made a slave of you, Mr. Bertram, and got you to do everything she wanted. She always does. She is a little witch," Lucy said.

"Oh, Tiny," said Bertram, with a slight change of color. "Yes—I had not been thinking. What is her—real name?"

"I believe it is Agnes, and another name too—an old-fashioned name; do you remember, mother?"

"Laetitia. I don't know what you mean by an old-fashioned name. I had once a great friend whose name was Laetitia. It means light-heartedness, doesn't it?—joy. And a very nice meaning, too. It would just suit Tiny. They can call her Letty when she gets a little older. But the worst of these baby names is that there is no getting rid of them; and Tiny is so absurd for a big girl."

During this rather long speech Bertram sat with a strange look, as if he could have cried, Lucy thought, which, however, must have been absurd, for what he did do was to laugh. "Yes, they do stick; and the more absurd they are the longer they last."

"Tiny, however, is not absurd in the least; and isn't she a delightful little thing?" Lucy repeated. She was not, perhaps, though so very good a girl, very rapid in her perceptions, and besides, it would have been entirely idiotic to imagine the existence of any reason why Bertram should not discuss freely the little characteristics of Mrs. Nugent's child.

"Poor little Tiny!" he said, quite inappropriately, with a sort of stifled sigh.

"Oh! do you mean because her father is dead?" said Lucy, with a countenance of dismay. She blamed herself immediately for having thought so little of that misfortune. Perhaps the thing was that Mr. Bertram had been a friend of Tiny's father, and it was this that made him so grave. She added, "I am sure I am very sorry for poor Mr. Nugent; but then I never knew him, or knew anybody that knew him. Yes, to be sure, poor little Tiny! But, Mr. Bertram, she has such a very nice mother. Don't you think for a girl the most important thing is to have a nice mother?"

"No doubt," Bertram said very gravely, and again he sighed.

Lucy was full of compunction, but scarcely knew how to express it. He must have been a very great friend of poor Mr. Nugent, and perhaps he had felt, seeing Nelly quite out of mourning, and looking on the whole so bright, that his friend had been forgotten. But no! Lucy was ready to go to the stake for it, that Mrs. Nugent had not forgotten her husband—more at least than it was inevitable and kind to her other friends to forget.

And then Mr. Wradisley, having finished his complaints about "your cook," told his mother across the table that it was quite possible he might have to go to town in a few days. "Perhaps to-morrow," he said. The dealer in antiquities, through whose hands he spent a great deal of money, had some quite unique examples which it would be sinful to let slip by.

Mrs. Wradisley exclaimed against this suggestion. "I thought, Reginald, you were to be at home with us all the winter; and Ralph just come, too," she said.

"Oh, don't mind me," said Ralph.

"Ralph may be sure, mother," said Mr. Wradisley, with his usual dignity, "that I mind him very much. Still there are opportunities that occur but once in a lifetime. But nothing," he added, "need be settled till to-morrow."

What did Reginald expect to-morrow? Mr. Bertram looked up too with a sort of involuntary movement, as if he were about to say something concerning to-morrow; but then changed his mind and did not speak. This was Lucy's observation, who was uneasy, watching them all, and feeling commotion, though she knew not whence it came, in the air.

In the morning there was still the same commotion in the air to Lucy's consciousness, who perhaps, however, was the only person who was aware of it. But any vague sensation of that sort was speedily dispersed by the exclamation of Mrs. Wradisley, after she had poured out the tea and coffee (which was an office she retained in her own hands, to Lucy's indignation). While she did this she glanced at the outside of the letters which lay by the side of her plate; for they retained the bad habit in Wradisbury of giving you your letters at breakfast, instead of sending them up to your room as soon as they arrived; so that you received your tailor's bill or your lover's letter before the curious eyes of all the world, so to speak. Mrs. Wradisley looked askance at her letters as she poured out the tea, and said, half to herself, "Ah! Mrs. Nugent. Now what can she be writing to me about? I saw her last night, and I shall probably see her to-day."

"It will be about those cuttings for the garden, mother," said Lucy. "May I open it and see?"

Mrs. Wradisley put her hand for a moment on the little pile. "I prefer to open my letters myself. No one has ever done that for me yet."

"Nor made the tea either, mother," said Ralph.

"Nor made the tea either, Raaf, though Lucy would like to put me out, I know," said Mrs. Wradisley, with a little nod of her head; and then, having finished that piece of business like one who felt her very life attacked by any who should question her powers of doing it, she proceeded to open her letters—one or two others before that on which she had remarked.

Lucy was so much interested herself that she did not see how still her elder brother sat behind his paper, or how uneasy Bertram was, cutting his roll into small pieces on his plate. Then Mrs. Wradisley gave a little scream, and gave them all an excuse for looking up at her, and Mr. Wradisley for demanding, "What is the matter, mother?" in his quiet tones.

"Dear me! I beg your pardon, Reginald, for crying out; how very absurd of me. Mrs. Nugent has gone away! I was so startled I could not help it. She's gone away! This is to tell me—and she was here all the afternoon yesterday, and never said a word."

"Oh, that's the little widow," said Ralph; "and a very good thing too, I should say, mother. Nothing so dangerous as little widows about."

Again I am sorry that Lucy was so much absorbed in her own emotions as not to be capable of general observation, or she would have seen that both her brother Reginald and Mr. Bertram looked at Raaf as if they would like to cut his throat.

"She says she did tell me yesterday," said Mrs. Wradisley, reading her letter. "'I mentioned that I had news that disturbed me a little.' Yes, now I recollect she did. I thought she wasn't looking herself, and of course I asked what was the matter. But I had forgotten all about it, and I never thought it was serious. 'And now I find that I must go. You have all been so kind to me, and I am so sorry to leave. Tiny, too, will break her little heart; only a child always believes she is coming back again to-morrow; and the worst of it is I don't know when I may be able to get back.'"

"But, mother, she can't have gone yet; there will be time to run and say good-by by the ten o'clock train," said Lucy, getting up hurriedly.

Once more Mrs. Wradisley raised a restraining hand, "Listen," she said, "you've not heard the end. 'To-night I am going up to town by the eight o'clock train. I have not quite settled what my movements will be afterwards; but you shall hear when I know myself.' That's all," said the mother, "and very unsatisfactory I call it; but you see you will do no manner of good, Lucy, jumping up and disturbing everybody at breakfast on account of the ten o'clock train."

"Well," said Lucy, drawing a long breath, "that is something at least—if she will really let us know as soon as she knows herself."

"Gammon," said Ralph. "My belief is you will never hear of your pretty widow again. She's seen somebody that is up to her tricks, or she's broken down in some little game, or—"

"Raaf!" cried mother and sister together.

But that was not all. Mr. Wradisley put down his newspaper; his countenance appeared from behind it a little white and drawn, with his eyebrows lowering. "I am sorry, indeed," he said, "to hear a man of my name speak of a lady he knows nothing about as perhaps—a cad might speak, but not a gentleman."

"Reginald!" the ladies cried now in chorus, with tones of agitation and dismay.

Meanwhile Bertram had got up from the table with a disregard of good manners of which in the tumult of his feelings he was quite unconscious, and stalked away, going out of the room and the house, his head thrust forward as if he did not quite realize where he was going. The ladies afterwards, when they discussed this incident, and had got over their terror lest hot words should ensue between the brothers, as for the moment seemed likely—gave Bertram credit for the greatest tact and delicacy; since it was evident that he too thought a crisis was coming, and would not risk the chance of being a spectator of a scene which no stranger to the family ought to see.

But none of these fine sentiments were in Bertram's mind. He went out, stumbling as he went, because a high tide of personal emotion had surged up in him, swelling to his very brain. That may not be a right way to describe it, because they say all feeling comes from the brain—but that was how he felt. He scarcely heard the jabberings of these Wradisley people, who knew nothing about it. He who was the only man who had anything to say in the matter, to defend her or to assail her—he would have liked to knock down that fellow Ralph; but he would have liked still more to kick Ralph's brother out of the way, who had taken upon him to interfere and stand up for her, forsooth, as if he knew anything about her, whereas it was he, only he, Frank Bertram, who knew. He went staggering out of the house, but shook himself up when he got into the open air, and pulled himself together. There had been such a strong impulse upon him to go after her last night and seize hold upon her, to tell her all this was folly and nonsense, and couldn't be. Why had he not done it? He couldn't tell. To think that was his own child that he had carried about, and that after all she had been called Laetitia, after his mother, though her mother had cut him off and banished him for no immediate fault of his. It was his fault, but it was the fault of ignorance, not of intention. He had believed what he had so intently wished to be true, but he had no more meant to harm Nelly or her child than to sully the sunshine or the skies. And now, when chance or providence, or whatever you chose to call it, had brought them within sight of each other again, that he should not have had the heart to follow that meeting out at once, and insist upon his rights! Perhaps she would not have denied him—he had thought for a moment that there had been something in her eyes—and then, like the dolt he was, like the coward he was, he had let her go, and had gone in to dinner, and had sat through the evening and listened to their talk and their music, and had gone to bed and tossed and dreamed all night, and let her go. There had been impulses in him against all these things. He had thought of excusing himself from dinner. He had thought of pretending a headache, and stealing out later; but he had not done it. He had stuck there in their infernal routine, and let her go. Oh, what a dolt and coward slave am I! He would not put forth a hand to hold her, to clutch her, not a finger! But began to bestir himself as soon as she was out of his reach and had got clear away.

He went straight on toward the gate and the village, not much thinking where he was going, nor meaning anything in particular by it; but before he was aware found himself at Greenbank, where he had stopped once in the darkness, all unaware who was within, and listened to Ralph Wradisley (the cad! his brother was right) bringing forth his foolish rubbish about the pretty widow, confound him! And some one had asked him if perhaps he knew the Nugents, and he had said, Yes; but they were old people. Yes, he knew some Nugents, he had said. They had only been her grandparents, that was all. It was her mother's name she had taken, but he never guessed it, never divined it, though Tiny had divined it when she suddenly grew silent in his hands and gave him that look. Tiny had recognized him, like a shot! Though she had never seen him, though she was only five weeks old when—But he had not known her, had not known anything, nor how to behave himself when Providence placed such an unlooked for chance in his hands.

He went up to the house, the door of which stood wide open, and went in. All the doors were open with a visible emptiness, and that look of mute disorder and almost complaint which a deserted house bears when its inmates have gone away. A woman came out of the back regions on hearing his step, and explained that she had acted as Mrs. Nugent's cook, but was the caretaker put in by the landlord, and let or not with the house as might suit the inmate. Mrs. Nugent had behaved very handsome to her, she said, with wages and board wages, and to Lizzie too, the housemaid, who had gone back to her mother's, and refused to stay and help to clean out the house. It was out of order, as Mrs. Nugent only went last night; but if the gentleman would like to see over it—Bertram behaved handsome to her also, bidding her not trouble herself, and then was permitted to wander through the house at his will. There was nothing to be seen anywhere which had any association either to soothe or hurt his excited mind—a broken doll, an old yellow novel, a chair turned over in one room, the white coverlet in another twisted as if packing of some sort had been performed upon it—nothing but the merest vulgar traces of a sudden going away. In the little drawing-room there were some violets in water in a china cup—he remembered that she had worn them yesterday—and by their side and on the carpet beneath two or three of the forget-me-nots he had gathered for Tiny. He had almost thought of taking some of the violets (which was folly) away with him. But when he saw the forget-me-nots he changed his mind, and left them as he found them. His flowers had not found favor in her sight, it appeared! It was astonishing how much bitterness that trivial circumstance added to his feelings. He went out by the open window, relieved to get into the open air again, and went round and round the little garden, finding here and there play places of Tiny, where a broken toy or two, and some daisies threaded for a chain, betrayed her. And then it suddenly occurred to him that there were but two or three forget-me-nots, which might easily have fallen from Tiny's hot little hand, whereas there had been a large number gathered. What had been done with the rest? Had they by any possibility been carried away? The thought came with a certain balm to his heart. He said Folly! to himself, but yet there was a consolation in the thought.

He was seated on the rude little bench where Tiny had played, looking at her daisies, when he heard a step; and, looking through the hedge of lilac bushes which enclosed him, he saw to his great surprise Mr. Wradisley walking along the little terrace upon which the drawing-room windows opened. Mr. Wradisley could not be stealthy, that was impossible, but his step was subdued; and if anything could have made his look furtive, as if he were afraid of being seen, that would have been his aspect. He walked up and down the little terrace once or twice, and then he went in softly by the open window. In another moment he reappeared. He was carefully straightening out in his hands the limp forget-me-nots which had fallen from the table to the carpet out (no doubt) of Tiny's little hot hands. Mr. Wradisley took out a delicate pocket-book bound in morocco, and edged with silver, and with the greatest care, as if they had been the most rare specimens, arranged in it the very limp and faded flowers. Then he placed the book in his breast-pocket, and turned away. Bertram, in the little damp arbor, laid himself upon the bench to suppress the tempest of laughter which tore him in two. It was more like a convulsion than a fit of merriment, for laughter is a tragic expression sometimes, and it came to an end very abruptly in something not unlike a groan. Mr. Wradisley was already at some distance, but he stopped involuntarily at the sound of this groan, and looked back, but seeing nothing to account for it, walked on again at his usual dignified pace, carrying Tiny's little muddy, draggled forget-me-nots over his heart.

It was not till some time after that Bertram followed him up to the hall. He had neither taken Nelly's violets nor Tiny's daisies, though he had looked at them both with feelings which half longed for and half despised such poor tokens of the two who had fled from him. The thought of poor Mr. Wradisley's mistake gave him again and again a spasm of inaudible laughter as he went along the winding ways after him. After all, was it not a willful mistake, a piece of false sentiment altogether? for the man might have remembered, he said to himself, that Nelly wore violets, autumn violets, and not forget-me-nots. When he got to the house, Bertram found, as he had expected, a telegram summoning him to instant departure. He had taken means to have it sent when he passed through the village. And the same afternoon went away, offering many regrets for the shortness of his visit.

"Three days—a poor sort of Saturday to Monday affair," said Mrs. Wradisley. "You must come again and give us the rest that is owing to us."

"It is just my beastly luck," Bertram said.

As for Lucy, she tried to throw a great deal of meaning into her eyes as she bade him good-by; but Bertram did not in the least understand what the meaning was. He had an uncomfortable feeling for the moment, as if it might be that Lucy's heart had been touched, unluckily, as her brother's had been; but grew hot all over with shame, looking again at her innocent, intent face though what was in it, it was not given to him to read. What Lucy would have said had she dared would have been, "Oh, Mr. Bertram, go home to your wife and live happy ever after!" but this of course she had no right to say. Ralph, however, the downright, whom no one suspected of tact or delicacy, said something like it as he walked with his friend to the station. Or rather it was at the very last moment as he shook hands through the window of the railway carriage.

"Good-by, Bertram," he said; "I'd hunt up Mrs. Bertram and make it up, if I were you. Things like that can't go on forever, don't you know."

"There's something in what you say, Wradisley," Bertram replied.


## Margaret Oliphant – A Short Biography

Margaret Oliphant Wilson was born on April 4th, 1828 to Francis W. Wilson, a clerk, and Margaret Oliphant, at Wallyford, near Musselburgh, East Lothian.

She spent her childhood at Lasswade, near Dalkeith, Glasgow before moving to Liverpool.

Her youth was spent in establishing a writing style so much so that, in 1849, she had her first novel published: Passages in the Life of Mrs. Margaret Maitland based on the Scottish Free Church movement. It met with some success and was a good start to her career.

Two years later, in 1851, her third book Caleb Field was published. It was also now that she met the publisher William Blackwood in Edinburgh and was asked to contribute to his well-received Blackwood's Magazine. It was to be a lifelong endeavor. Over the course of the relationship she would have well over 100 articles published.

In May 1852, Margaret married her cousin, Frank Wilson Oliphant, at Birkenhead, and they settled at Harrington Square, Camden, London. He was an artist working primarily in stained glass. With the marriage she became Margaret Oliphant Wilson Oliphant.

Their marriage produced six children but three tragically died in infancy.

When her husband developed signs of the dreaded consumption (tuberculosis) they moved, on the advice of doctors, to warmer climes. In January 1859 it was to Florence, and then to Rome where, sadly, he died.

Margaret was naturally devastated but was also now left without support and only her income from her writing. She returned to England and took up the task of supporting her three remaining children by her literary activity.

By now she was being published both as an established novelist and regularly in Blackwood's Magazine, amongst several others. Her incredible and prolific work rate increased both her commercial reputation and the size of her reading audience.

Against this her domestic life continued to be tragic, full of sorrow and disappointment.

In January 1864 her only remaining daughter, Maggie, died and was buried in her father's grave in Rome. Her brother, who had emigrated to Canada, was shortly afterwards involved in financial ruin. Margaret generously offered a home to him and his children, adding another demand to her already heavy responsibilities.

In 1866 she settled at Windsor to be closer to her sons, who were being educated at near-by Eton School. That year, her second cousin, Annie Louisa Walker, came to live with her as a companion-housekeeper. Windsor was now to be her home for the rest of her life.

Her literary career for three decades was one of constant delivery and success. Whether she wrote historical works or across several genres in fiction: domestic realism, historical, romance or supernatural she was successful.

For more than thirty years she pursued a varied literary career but family life continued to bring problems.

The literary ambitions she wished for her sons were unfulfilled. Cyril Francis, the eldest, died in 1890, leaving a Life of Alfred de Musset, which was later incorporated in his mother's Foreign Classics for English Readers. The younger, Francis, who she nicknamed 'Cecco', collaborated with her in the Victorian Age of English Literature and won a position at the British Museum, but was rejected by Sir Andrew Clark, a famous physician. Cecco died in 1894.

With the last of her children now lost to her, she had but little further interest in life. Her health steadily and inexorably declined.

Margaret Oliphant Wilson Oliphant died at the age of 69 in Wimbledon on 20th June 1897. She is buried in Eton beside her sons.

At her death, Margaret was still working on Annals of a Publishing House, a record of Blackwood's Magazine with which she had enjoyed such a successful relationship.

Her Autobiography and Letters, which present a thoughtful picture of her domestic anxieties, was published in 1899. Only parts were written with a wider audience in mind: she had originally intended the Autobiography for her son, but he died before she could finish it.

Opinions on Oliphant's work are split, with some critics seeing her as a 'domestic novelist', while others recognize her work as influential and important to the Victorian literature canon. Critical reception from her contemporaries is also divided. John Skelton took the view that Oliphant wrote too much and too quickly. Writing a Blackwood's article called 'A Little Chat About Mrs. Oliphant', he asked, "Had Mrs. Oliphant concentrated her powers, what might she not have done? We might have had another Charlotte Brontë or another George Eliot." However not all of the contemporary reception was negative. The esteemed M. R. James admired Oliphant's supernatural fiction, concluding that "the religious ghost story, as it may be called, was never done better than by Mrs. Oliphant in 'The Open Door' and 'A Beleaguered City'. Mary Butts lavished praise on Oliphant's ghost story 'The Library Window', describing it as "one masterpiece of sober loveliness".

More modern critics of Oliphant's work include Virginia Woolf, who asked in 'Three Guineas' whether Oliphant's autobiography does not lead the reader "to deplore the fact that Mrs. Oliphant sold her brain, her very admirable brain, prostituted her culture and enslaved her intellectual liberty in order that she might earn her living and educate her children."

Whatever the merits of their cases Margaret Oliphant has been shamefully neglected in modern years. She is now becoming more widely recognised as a leading writer of her day.


Margaret Oliphant – A Concise Bibliography

A canon of more than 120 works, including novels, travel books, histories, and volumes of literary criticism.

Novels
Margaret Maitland (1849)
Merkland (1850)
Caleb Field (1851)
John Drayton (1851)
Adam Graeme (1852)
The Melvilles (1852)
Katie Stewart (1852)
Harry Muir (1853)
Ailieford (1853)
The Quiet Heart (1854)
Magdalen Hepburn (1854)
Zaidee (1855)
Lilliesleaf (1855)
Christian Melville (1855)

The Athelings (1857)
The Days of My Life (1857)
Orphans (1858)
The Laird of Norlaw (1858)
Agnes Hopetoun's Schools and Holidays (1859)
Lucy Crofton (1860)
The House on the Moor (1861)
The Last of the Mortimers (1862)
Heart and Cross (1863)
Salem Chapel (1863)
The Rector (1863)
Doctor's Family (1863)
The Perpetual Curate (1864)
Miss Marjoribanks (1866)
Phoebe Junior (1876)
A Son of the Soil (1865)
Agnes (1866)
Madonna Mary (1867)
Brownlows (1868)
The Minister's Wife (1869)
The Three Brothers (1870)
John: A Love Story (1870)
Squire Arden (1871)
At his Gates (1872)
Ombra (1872
May (1873)
Innocent (1873)
The Story of Valentine and His Brother (1875)
A Rose in June (1874)
For Love and Life (1874)
Whiteladies (1875)
An Odd Couple (1875)
The Curate in Charge (1876)
Carità (1877)
Young Musgrave (1877)
Mrs. Arthur (1877)
The Primrose Path (1878)
Within the Precincts (1879)
The Fugitives (1879)
A Beleaguered City (1879)
The Greatest Heiress in England (1880)
He That Will Not When He May (1880)
In Trust (1881)
Harry Joscelyn (1881)
Lady Jane (1882)
A Little Pilgrim in the Unseen (1882)
The Lady Lindores (1883)
Sir Tom (1883)

Hester (1883)
It Was a Lover and his Lass (1883)
The Lady's Walk (1883)
The Wizard's Son (1884)
Madam (1884)
The Prodigals and Their Inheritance (1885)
Oliver's Bride (1885)
A Country Gentleman and His Family (1886)
A House Divided Against Itself (1886)
Effie Ogilvie (1886)
A Poor Gentleman (1886)
The Son of His Father (1886)
Joyce (1888)
Cousin Mary (1888)
The Land of Darkness (1888)
Lady Car (1889)
Kirsteen (1890)
The Mystery of Mrs. Biencarrow (1890)
Sons and Daughters (1890)
The Railway Man and His Children (1891)
The Heir Presumptive and the Heir Apparent (1891)
The Marriage of Elinor (1891)
Janet (1891)
The Cuckoo in the Nest (1892)
Diana Trelawny (1892)
The Sorceress (1893)
A House in Bloomsbury (1894)
Sir Robert's Fortune (1894)
Who Was Lost and is Found (1894)
Lady William (1894)
Two Strangers (1895)
Old Mr. Tredgold (1895)
The Unjust Steward (1896)
The Ways of Life (1897)


Short stories
Neighbours on the Green (1889)
A Widow's Tale and Other Stories (1898)
That Little Cutty (1898)
The Open Door (1918)


Selected Articles
Mary Russel Mitford (Blackwood's Magazine, Vol. 75, 1854)
Evelin and Pepys (Blackwood's Magazine, Vol. 76, 1854)
The Holy Land (Blackwood's Magazine, Vol. 76, 1854)
Mr. Thackeray and his Novels (Blackwood's Magazine, Vol. 77, 1855)

Bulwer (Blackwood's Magazine, Vol. 77, 1855)
Charles Dickens (Blackwood's Magazine, Vol. 77, 1855)
Modern Novelists—Great and Small (Blackwood's Magazine, Vol. 77, 1855)
Modern Light Literature: Poetry (Blackwood's Magazine, Vol. 79, 1856)
Religion in Common Life (Blackwood's Magazine, Vol. 79, 1856)
Sydney Smith (Blackwood's Magazine, Vol. 79, 1856)
The Laws Concerning Women (Blackwood's Magazine, Vol. 79, 1856)
The Art of Caviling (Blackwood's Magazine, Vol. 80, 1856)
Béranger (Blackwood's Magazine, Vol. 83, 1858)
The Condition of Women (Blackwood's Magazine, Vol. 83, 1858)
The Missionary Explorer (Blackwood's Magazine, Vol. 83, 1858)
Religious Memoirs (Blackwood's Magazine, Vol. 83, 1858)
Social Science (Blackwood's Magazine, Vol. 88, 1860)
Scotland and her Accusers (Blackwood's Magazine, Vol. 90, 1861)
The Chronicles of Carlingford (Blackwood's Magazine 1862–1865)
Girolamo Savonarola (Blackwood's Magazine, Vol. 93, 1863)
The Life of Jesus (Blackwood's Magazine, Vol. 96, 1864)
Giacomo Leopardi (Blackwood's Magazine, Vol. 98, 1865)
The Great Unrepresented (Blackwood's Magazine, Vol. 100, 1866)
Mill on the Subjection of Women (The Edinburgh Review, Vol. 130, 1869)
The Opium-Eater (Blackwood's Magazine, Vol. 122, 1877)
Russian and Nihilism in the Novels of I. Tourgeniéf (Blackwood's Magazine, Vol. 127, 1880)
School and College (Blackwood's Magazine, Vol. 128, 1880)
The Grievances of Women (Fraser's Magazine, New Series, Vol. 21, 1880)
Mrs. Carlyle (The Contemporary Review, Vol. 43, May 1883)
The Ethics of Biography (The Contemporary Review, July 1883)
Victor Hugo (The Contemporary Review, Vol. 48, July/December 1885)
A Venetian Dynasty (The Contemporary Review, Vol. 50, August 1886)
Laurence Oliphant (Blackwood's Magazine, Vol. 145, 1889)
Tennyson (Blackwood's Magazine, Vol. 152, 1892)
Addison, the Humorist (Century Magazine, Vol. 48, 1894)
The Anti-Marriage League (Blackwood's Magazine, Vol. 159, 1896)


Biographies
Edward Irving (1862)
Francis of Assisi (1871)
Count de Montalembert (1872)
Dante (1877)
Cervantes (1880)
Life of Sheridan in the English Men of Letters series (1883)
John Tulloch (1888)
Laurence Oliphant (1892)


Historical & Critical Works
Historical Sketches of the Reign of George II (1869)
The Makers of Florence (1876)

A Literary History of England from 1760 to 1825 (1882)
The Makers of Venice (1887)
Royal Edinburgh (1890)
Jerusalem (1891)
The Makers of Modern Rome (1895)
William Blackwood and his Sons (1897)
The Sisters Brontë. In: Women Novelists of Queen Victoria's Reign (1897)

www.ingramcontent.com/pod-product-compliance
Lightning Source LLC
Chambersburg PA
CBHW061502170626
46811CB00004B/1593